CRAZY WEATHER

THE MACMILLAN COMPANY
NEW YORK · BOSTON · CHICAGO
DALLAS · ATLANTA · SAN FRANCISCO

CRAZY

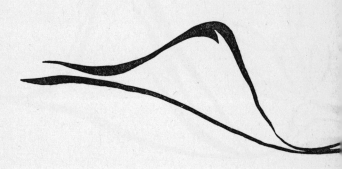

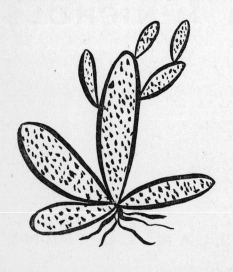

WEATHER

CHARLES L. McNICHOLS

NEW YORK, 1944

THE MACMILLAN COMPANY

PRINTED AND BOUND IN THE U. S. A. BY
KINGSPORT PRESS, INC., KINGSPORT, TENN.

CONTENTS

CRAZY WEATHER

Chapter I

CRAZY WEATHER

On a morning in late August, in the fourteenth year and seventh month of his life, South Boy awoke and found himself between two beehives under the low fronds of a thrifty young fan palm. He lay still for nearly a minute before he grudgingly stretched his heavy, aching limbs. Then he yawned with a yawn that cracked his jaw hinges. A vague sense of uneasiness added to his discomfort, but for some time he couldn't determine the cause of it.

True, it was late to be just waking up. The slant of a sunbeam laden with dancing dust particles told him the sun was nearly two hours high. But time had never been any concern of South Boy's. So he lay and listened, his heart beating slow and in instinctive apprehension, his eyes rolling, cautiously taking in everything within the narrow limits of his sleeping quarters. They rested at the entrance of one of the hives. There was no traffic to and fro. A small, restless swarm buzzed about the entrance, wings fanning furiously. From within that hive and the other came a deeper, muffled buzzing that was almost like the sound of gourd rattles shaken furiously, far off. The bees were desperately fanning air to their young.

"I know what's the matter," said South Boy, getting up. "It's hot!"

He ducked out into the blinding, stunning glare of the sun and headed for the olla that hung in the grape arbor alongside the summer kitchen.

One gourd of cold water in his stomach and another doused over his head chased away the dim half-dread, and he reached up and snipped off a bunch of brown-ripe, sugar-sweet muscats

1

and began methodically popping the grapes into his mouth, shivering delightedly as the water that dripped from his rope-colored, half-long hair trickled inside the open collar of his faded blue shirt and ran down his spine. Thus, for several minutes he enjoyed himself—eating, shivering, staring at the damp, burlap-wrapped water jar, wondering about what sort of miracle it wrought in making the water within it so much colder than the air without. Someone had told him "evaporation," but he was still asking himself "Why?"

He glanced over at the big spirit thermometer hanging in the deepest shade against the canvas lower wall of the summer kitchen and shook his head when he saw that the column of red liquid stood at 110. At noon, a temperature of a hundred and ten would have been nothing to remark about, but at seven in the morning—South Boy said "Uh-huh, hot!" He began listening for small noises that should be heard at that time in the morning, but there were none. The world about was already wrapped in the dead, heavy silence brought about by the desert's midday heat.

From inside the kitchen a querulous voice called, "Chico?"

"Hi!" croaked South Boy.

"Vente! Vente!" the voice cracked angrily.

"Vengo, ya," grumbled South Boy; and then he said to himself in English, "I bet a short-bit we're in for a spell of crazy weather!" and tossed away the grape stem.

It was stifling in the screen-and-canvas summer kitchen. South Boy let the screen door slam just to relieve the untimely stillness and sat down at the near end of a long plank table. A huge Mexican woman in a gray wrapper, the sweat streaming down her fat face, flounced angrily over to the stove, dumped tepid, soggy flapjacks and limp bacon from a frying pan onto a chipped enamel plate, and slid it down the length of the table before she slopped a crockery cup full of coffee from a gallon pot.

South Boy reached for the syrup. The cook slumped down

into her old rocker by the stove and glared at him. He knew why she was angry. She was a creature of habit and never left the kitchen until all the men had been fed; so, waiting for him, she'd sat there and stewed when she might have been under the shade of her favorite willow by the main irrigating ditch since sunup if he'd have come to breakfast at the regular time. He knew if she'd been a white woman or a Mojave she'd have hunted him up long ago and given him a jawing for keeping her waiting. But this woman came from some obscure, subjected race down on the Mexican plateau—a people that had been serfs of the Spaniards for four hundred years and serfs of unknown red masters for generations before that. So she didn't speak out, but glowered and sulked and chewed on her grievance after the manner of the downtrodden, and brooded over some devious retaliation in the depth of her mind like a hen owl brooding over her eggs.

It came to South Boy then that he should say something to excuse himself for the inconvenience he had caused her. He would have said it, too, if she had been able to understand English or Mojave; but the heat made his mind too lazy to think up the appropriate Mexican phrases. Instead it slipped easily into making and rejecting plans for his day as he sopped up syrup with sections of flapjack.

He thought of twisting a new hair rope, or cleaning his saddle, or going fishing, or hunting up his old friend the trapper, called the Mormonhater; but he rejected each of these ideas as it came up: Too much work . . . Too much traveling . . . The Mormonhater might be hard to find. His boat hadn't been seen in the near stretches of the river for a couple of months . . .

Just as he wiped up the last of the syrup with the last leathery sop, the cook broke out with a mirthless, cackling giggle. He looked up to see a fat forefinger pointed at his head.

"Bonitos—cabellos—lar-r-rgos," she droned with a slow exaggeration of *dega* dialect of the peon that denoted heavy sarcasm. South Boy batted his eyes and chewed methodically, trying to figure out what she was up to.

"Un otro Boofalo Beel, como El Bravo!" she continued, staring at South Boy with sullen expectancy. South Boy stared back at her complacently, mumbling over her words. "Pretty long hair. Another Buffalo Bill, like El Bravo," she said in a tone that was deliberately insulting.

He knew El Bravo, the Tough Guy, was her name for her husband, a moody and combative exile from Texas who bossed the ranch when South Boy's father wasn't around to do his own bossing. He knew that El Bravo wore his hair down to his shoulders and that on the wall of his bedroom, where he could see it every morning when he awoke, he had tacked a signed photograph of Colonel Cody. Not that he admired the Colonel so much; in fact he said publicly that he could out-shoot, outride, and even outdrink Bill Cody any time. South Boy had heard him make the statement. The Foreman had kept the picture as a symbol of what might have been. For El Bravo was once well on the way to becoming a celebrated Western Character himself.

He'd been a trail driver, a ranger, a valiant fighter against the Apache and the Comanche, and a rare shot with a rifle and pistol. About the time when Colonel Cody was making head-lines with the European tour of his Wild West Show, certain men of money decided to put El Bravo on the road with a show of his own. But it so happened that on the eve of the launching of the enterprise, El Bravo had to kill one of the backers of his show, a person of wide family connections and considerable political influence.

So El Bravo rode for Arizona with vengeance on his heels, and instead of becoming the darling of the crowds in the East and in Europe entertained by duchesses and such, he went on a prolonged drunk in Prescott and woke up legally married to this Mexican woman. Now he was working on a little two-by-four ranch—his own description—married to a hay bag he was shamed to take to Needles, even.

All this South Boy knew very well, because the Foreman had often told him. He didn't know that the Hay Bag had long since discovered that she could avenge herself upon her husband by simply pointing her finger at him and drawling, "Como Boofalo Beel, no?" Sometimes he would brood for days afterwards. South Boy didn't understand that she expected the same reaction from any other long-haired male. So he just blinked at her, puzzled.

"Como Boofalo Beel, no?" she cried, her voice rising.

Then she did what the daughters of the downtrodden never do except in last desperation. She resorted to violence. She seized the pot off the stove and threw it at South Boy.

South Boy, who was through eating, ducked the pot handily and dived out through the door. He paused for a moment under the grape arbor and listened to the turmoil of dish-smashing going on within. He glanced at the red column of the thermometer—114, and rising.

"Yep, crazy weather," he said. "And it's sure got ol' Hay Bag."

He'd discarded all ideas of doing anything interesting that day and decided he would try reading. So he walked over to the ranch house, got down on his belly, and crawled under the back gallery where the space between the floor and the ground was too limited to admit anyone but himself and the house cat. Back about six or eight feet was a small depression where the cat had her semiannual litter of kittens and South Boy kept his personal cache. Thence he took an old copy of Bob Ingersoll's lectures that had remained unread since the Mormonhater had loaned it to him in the spring, and slowly backing out into the sunlight and shading his eyes with the book, he returned to his sleeping place under the palm tree.

There he sat with his back against the rough bole of the tree, idly turning the pages. The book didn't look very interesting. He had only consented to take it home in the first place because of the divergent opinions the Mormonhater and his mother had expressed about Mr. Ingersoll. His mother said he was the Devil's disciple. The Mormonhater said he was the smartest man ever born.

South Boy had been aiming to find out why for a long time, but until now his days had been too full. Now he tried hard to find out whatever there was great or devilish in the first few lines, but the sweat ran into his eyes and blinded him. The bees, in their desperate attempt to air-condition their breeding chambers, were making too much noise. And without warning South Boy began to be bothered about his hair. It had grown long, or "half-long," as the Mojaves say, simply because since his mother was gone no one had taken the trouble to say, "Cut the boy's hair." As for his part, it was easier to let it grow than to get it cut. He never thought about it until the Mexican woman set the seeds of thinking in the back of his head.

A moment or two of fretful annoyance and he slammed the book down and again ducked out into the glare. I reckon it ain't too hot to go see Havek, he thought, picturing the airy shade under Havek's mother's willow-roof, where he could lie on the dampened, hard-packed adobe floor and gossip and sleep all day with Havek and his various relatives. Maybe by night it would be cool enough to go fishing.

The sun struck him like a ponderous weight and pressed down on him from all sides, but he walked quickly because the hot, white dust burnt through a quarter-inch of callus and stung his feet. The nearest relief was the shade of the west side of the stack of baled hay in the center of the horse corral. He rolled over the willow-pole fence and ran for it, his mouth open and his eyes glazed. Once in the shadow of the stack he squatted on his heels, panting.

There were a dozen saddle horses in a single file, some head to head, some nose to tail, leaning against the stack, for the hay was still several degrees cooler than the air. South Boy felt no inclination to go out into the sun again to find a saddle or bridle, so he kicked through the litter underfoot until he found an old piece of stake rope, and walking up to the nearest animal—she happened to be a dun mare with a brown stripe the length of her back—he had the rope tied around her neck and a half-hitch bent around her nose before she roused out of her daze.

South Boy heaved himself onto her back and clamped fast with his knees, drumming his heels against her fat sides to drive her away from the stack. The mare stood the drumming for a full minute as though she were debating whether it was worth the effort to try to buck him off, and then shook her head. She moved slowly away from the hay, with little steps. She walked past the other horses, so close that South Boy's nigh leg rubbed hard against several of them, and then out into the killing sun.

Near the end of the half-mile stretch of shadeless trail to the lower irrigation ditch the mare began to stagger. South Boy did his best to keep her on her feet but she fell right by the fringe of small willows at the edge of the ditch. He jumped free, slipped off the hackamore, and stood coiling the rope over his left hand and elbow, staring down at the mare with amazement. "What do you know! She foundered out on me! I ain't never seen the sun knock out a horse so soon!"

Up to this point he hadn't noticed any particular ill effects of the sun on himself except the usual discomfort of sweat that poured out and dried in a sticky salt rime all over his body. He did notice he was a little bit dizzy and a little bit frightened. Fortunately the ditch was running bank-full. He promptly dived headlong into it, rolled over, sat up chest-deep in the roily water, fetched up handfuls of cool red mud from the bottom and began plastering it over his head and the back of his neck.

"Good thing my hair is a little bit long," he said. "Damn sun might have killed me." He remembered he had been warned that the summer's sun would kill white people who didn't wear hats. He never wore a hat five weekdays in his life, so he hadn't believed it.

He sat thinking. "It's too far to Havek's, but it is only a half-mile to the river. The river water runs deep, and it's cooler than ditch water. I'll go to the river and stay there until the crazy weather is past."

He rose to his knees and looked over the bank at the mare. She lay still, her neck stretched out. She looked dead, but South Boy noticed she had fallen craftily, her head in the shade of the willows. He got out of the ditch, raised his left foot over her head and let about a pint of muddy water run out of the leg of his jeans and over her head.

The mare promptly scrambled to her feet; giving South Boy a look of infinite disgust, she bolted into the nearest mesquite without regarding its thorns, and there she stood, with only her defiant rump showing.

"No, I ain't going to try and dig you out of there," said South Boy, and he went slowly away toward the west, toward the *Colorado Grande*, dripping a twisting trail, for he traveled from the lacy shade of one mesquite tree to another for the relief of his feet.

There was a sort of boundary line by the river's bank where mesquite and gourd vines and soapweed gave way to current-scoured earth and big willows—big enough to have stood against the last high water—and at this place South Boy ran across the old man called Hook-a-row.

Time and heat had shriveled Hook-a-row to much less than the six feet, two hundred pounds that was the size of a Mojave man in his prime. But he still walked upright and struck his long staff at the ground with force and decision. He was a rather disreputable-looking old man. His long gray hair was not twisted into ropes in the Mojave way, but fell in a loose, untidy tangle to his shoulders, and there was a rag bound around his head Apache-fashion. He wore a dirty white man's

suit of ancient cut and a long undershirt that hung outside his
pants and almost to his knees. At the same time there was an
air of distinction about him that marked him as a man of quality and he showed his good manners in the courteous way he
greeted South Boy.

"Friend-of-mine."

South Boy said, "Old-man-my-uncle," which is the polite
way to greet a man of his age; and he added, "It's hot," in
English.

"Hot? Hot?" laughed Hook-a-row, as cheerfully as if it had
been a spring morning. He put his head a little to one side, like
an inquiring bird. He had something else on his mind, for while
he appeared to be trying to remember the meaning of the English word his sparsely bearded face lost its cheerfulness and
grew sadder and sadder until there were tears brimming in his
eyes.

"What's the matter?" asked South Boy.

"It's the matter of your half-long hair. There is tears in my
eyes because there is sorrow to your left, or so I hear. Nothing
was said and nothing was known, or we would have come and
cried at the proper time."

Stupid from the heat and still beset with the recurrent uneasiness that had troubled him since he first awoke, South Boy
shuffled his feet and pondered the old man's meaning. "Half-
long hair": that would be a sign of mourning to a Mojave. The
old man was referring to a death with the elaborate circum-
locution necessary to avoid giving offense. "To your left":
that meant on South Boy's mother's side.

South Boy cried, "Oh, no, she isn't dead. Truly. She went
away for doctoring by the ocean." South Boy's mother had
gone to Los Angeles for an operation eight months before.
"She was cured, but the doctor said she must stay there until
the hot weather breaks. You will see her back here by the
second full moon from now, or thereabouts."

Whereupon the old man laughed in great relief and wiped

his eyes with his dirty sleeve. He pointed to South Boy's mud-smeared hair. "Then that means nothing," he said.

"Nothing," said South Boy, thinking sullenly, First, the cook, then this old man . . . He added, "My hair has grown lately."

"Yes," said Hook-a-row. "Yes, truly. Maybe it grows all-the-way-long and it will be twisted into fifty strands and you will become a Real Person indeed."

He went away chuckling to himself, and South Boy went on down to the river, not knowing that more seeds of thought had been planted in the back of his mind.

There was a big black-willow that made shade over the water all day long at the spot where he came to the river's bank. And the river in those days was the old wild river, before any dams had tamed it. It was deep and strong, and its usual color was that of coffee with a spoonful of cream in it; but today it showed a strong tinge of red as it did when there had been big rains far away in the Navajo country causing the Little Colorado to dump a stinking red flood into the big river above the Grand Canyon.

So the river on this day not only was red, but was a foot higher than it had been the day before, and there was an added restlessness to its surge. South Boy heard it talking to him in disquieting tones. He stripped off his clothes, caked with ditch mud that had already dried, dropped them on the bank, and slid into the water.

By and by he crawled up the bank and into the first fork of the big willow, where such breeze as did come off the river cooled his wet skin. Against the sooty gray of the willow bark he made a motionless pattern of golden brown—the color of a new saddle freshly oiled. His back was against the downstream side of the fork, his right knee was braced against the upstream limb, and his left leg hung down the trunk.

For a moment he was almost happy, watching the river, wide and strong, its rolling sand boils and its ever-changing

pattern of crosscurrents and back currents. There was a great
sand bar out in the middle, dried bone-white in the two months
since the recession of the annual great flood. Over it the heat
waves danced frantically, distorting the line of green that was
the grove of willows and cottonwoods on the Nevada bank.
But in the heat and unaccustomed idleness, the seeds of thought
that had been planted in the back of his mind grew disturb-
ingly.

First, he frowned as he puzzled over the cook's talk about
his hair. Then he squirmed over Hook-a-row's mention of his
mother. So the Mojaves had decided she was dead. That was
why no one had asked about her lately.

Well, she'd be back by October, and he'd be very glad.

Truly, hadn't he always been waiting by the Needles road
each Tuesday and Saturday when the stage went by on its way
to Fort Mojave to collect her long letter? Didn't he read it to
his father whenever he was home and see to it his father wrote
an answer in time to make the down stage on Wednesdays and
Mondays? Didn't he always write her a full, honest page, himself, for every letter, and two pages when his father was not at
home?

Still, when she came back he would be confronted with Cultural Advancement and Christian Instruction again. And he
would hear the cry that grew in persistence every year. "When
are we sending this boy away to school?"

For South Boy's mother was not only a white woman, she
was a lady. She said herself she belonged to Another World.
Certainly she was no part of either of the two worlds around
her—these, according to her own description, were the Rough
World of the White Man and the Heathen World of the Indian. She had been forced by a fraud of nature to give South
Boy to the breast of an Indian woman, but almost from the day
he learned to drink cow's milk out of a glass she had sought to
armor him with Cultural Advancement and Christian Instruction against the Rough and the Heathen Worlds.

Every weekday South Boy received two hours of Cultural Advancement, which began with reading and writing when he was small and afterwards developed into two pages of Tarr and McMurry's "Advanced Geography," one chapter of Wells's "History of the United States," and two pages of "Gems of Great Literature," the first two to be memorized at least in part, and the latter to be read "with feeling and proper pronunciation." All this was no great chore for South Boy, who had all three volumes almost by heart within a year and had learned to think of more interesting things, like shooting ducks or wild pigs, while he was reciting.

At the end of the two hours he was turned over to his father, who spent fifteen or twenty minutes teaching him arithmetic and, lately, double entry bookkeeping—both of which he enjoyed. By that time his mother, always in delicate health, had retired to read in her own room; so South Boy sallied out into the Rough or the Heathen World, as suited his fancy, and learned all those things he had been armored against: from the Foreman; from various callous cowhands (most of them fugitives from something or other); from the Mormonhater; from the Yavapai roustabout; and from several score Mojaves, his most cherished companions.

Christian Instruction came on the long weary Sabbath. He read ten selected chapters out of the Bible—selected by his mother so he wouldn't run into any embarrassingly frank language—and one sermon, long, tough, and dry, by some Scotchman. On the Sundays they stayed at home he could escape after dinner, when his mother took a nap. On alternate Sundays he was stuck for all day. He had to hitch up his mother's surrey, drive around to the house for his mother and the cook, drive down to a point across the river from Needles, yell his lungs out to fetch the cable ferry, lead the skittish horses on and off the old flatboat—and carefully keep from cussing when they tried to jump into the river—drive the cook to the Catholic church, go with his mother to the Presbyterian mission, sit through a sermon, and then reverse all that tedium homeward.

All in his good clothes, too. The only bright spot on these days was when the rig would encounter a rattlesnake. As his mother loathed snakes and there was a biblical admonition against them, it was permissible for him to use the shotgun that he was allowed to carry in the rig for defense purposes only.

Usually he fired suddenly, scaring the wits out of his passengers and the horses. After he had checked the runaways and after the screams in the back seat had been reduced to gasps he would explain he had to shoot the snake without warning because it was coming to attack the horses.

Of course the cook never believed him, but his mother still thought a snake, no matter how far away it was, had murder on its mind. For all these years in the wilderness—her own term —she had lived in her own island of Culture and Civilization, hermetically sealed against the facts of the world without— Rough, Heathen or Herpetological.

Still, South Boy loved his mother. She was a dear, good woman. He missed her very much and he would be glad to give all his Sundays and two hours of every other day to have her back. It was the thought of being sent away to be shut up among white strangers in a school that made his skin prickle and the sweat beads form on his hands. As the day of her return approached, he had fought off thinking about it and had succeeded because he kept busy. Now that crazy weather enforced idleness he could fight it off no longer.

As though the thought of white strangers could conjure them up, the sound of voices talking English came floating down the river and after it came a good big boat with an awning rigged on willow poles and three white men under it, cursing the heat and dipping up hatfuls of water to pour over their perspiring heads. The boat drifted into the near channel.

"Hullo," said the man in the bow. There was a surveying transit leaning against the gunwale beside him. South Boy said to himself: "Strangers. Government men. What are they doing always gadding up and down the river? The Mormonhater says, 'The government's fixin' to do something to the river, and I bet, by damn, they ruin it!' "

As South Boy didn't answer him the white man said: "No savvy English. Must be one the school didn't catch."

The man in the stern said: "Must be a breed. He's two or three shades too light for a Mojave, and too thin."

"He's a Chemehuevi and on the wrong side of the river," said the man who lay across the thwarts amidships.

South Boy thought: Two or three years ago I'd have answered them; but I get so I like strangers less and less. Still, if I'm dressed and on horseback I stop and speak with strangers. And when I'm dressed and on a horse nobody but a tenderfoot would take me for an Indian.

Then he heard one of the men say, "Speaking of Chemehuevis, I wonder how the boys are making it up north with the Piutes?" Which meant nothing to South Boy at the time.

A big black horsefly lit on his arm. He slapped once and killed it. A little sweat bee buzzed by, and he slapped twice and it flew away. He found a gratifying release from the continuing and increasingly gnawing anxiety even in that small distraction. But there were no more insects. They died in crazy weather. Back in his mind the thought was running again: Sent away. Shut up with strangers! Three—four years—academy. Three—four years—college. Three—four years—divinity school. His mother wanted him to be a preacher.

He tried to find new distraction in counting the driftwood coming down the river, but pretty soon he was counting, "Nine years shut up, ten years shut up, eleven years . . ." This torment went on for some minutes, until a scattering of little logs came by in a bunch with a big log following, like a bunch of short yearlings being driven by a horseman.

And at the sight his heart bounded with hope. He remembered that his father grew silent and sulky whenever the go-away-to-school subject had been broached. Not that he ever said "No"; but it was certain that he didn't like the idea, particularly since South Boy had learned to be handy in keeping books and, to a lesser degree, in the regular routine work around the ranch.

Maybe, he thought, maybe when she comes back she won't be sickly any more, and we both can say No without worrying about how it will make her feel.

But it came to him then that if he approached his father in the matter of making a firm stand against the go-away-to-school he'd shake his big head solemnly and declare, "If I do that, you got to be more help around here. You got to take responsibilities."

South Boy had been hearing too much of that "take responsibilities" this last year. There had been a time when he could work with the men when he wanted to, and when work no longer interested him he could go away and find something that did. But a couple of years ago his father made the first talk about taking responsibilities and foisted onto him the biweekly church trips to Needles. Then it was the bookkeeping. Then it was the screw-fly patrol. Every newborn calf had to be found and have its navel doctored with antiseptic and pine-tar salve against screw-fly blow, so the screw-fly patrol was a tediously regular, unending job. It didn't take all of South Boy's time by any means, but it was another continuing curtailment of his freedom.

He had the Yavapai roustabout to help him; but the Yavapai was a hired hand and an Indian besides, and wasn't expected to take responsibilities. So if a newborn calf lay close under the low branches of a mesquite, as it usually did, it was South Boy who had to go into that mesquite. The Yavapai could pretend he didn't see the calf. It was South Boy's hide the thorns ripped while he got the calf out. It was South Boy who had to tie the calf and do the dirty work of doctoring while Yavapai got all the fun and excitement of fighting off the calf's furious, red-eyed, bawling mother with the end of his rope.

Sitting, watching the river, South Boy came to the definite decision that taking responsibilities meant taking on all the disagreeable jobs no one else wanted. "And the way they're piling up on me I won't have five minutes' time for fishing by a year from now."

Somewhere in the "Gems of Great Literature" there was something said about the horns of a dilemma. South Boy knew then that he was caught between Hard Work and Exile-and-Involuntary-Confinement just as sure as he was at that moment sitting between two great limbs of a black-willow tree.

Again came diversion. A big, gray, naked drift log was floating down the river, and on the middle of the log—stretched out belly down, his bandanna-wrapped head resting on a projecting snag that had been a root, one hand dangling down in the red-brown water, his clothes in a bundle on his broad back—rode a sun-blackened naked Mojave, singing a song about the Pleiades. Singing loud and full and hearty, as a mockingbird sings on a hot night.

The log swung in on the Arizona side of the sand bar. The Mojave saw South Boy, raised his head, and pointed his wet hand upstream and shouted something about "*Chemehuevi ah-way.*"

This second reference to Piutes certainly would have gained South Boy's immediate attention if he had been in anything like a normal state of mind. As it was, he raised his hand in a languid salute and turned his head to watch the log shoot over toward the sand bar as it caught a sudden crosscurrent. The Mojave dropped his hand into the water and once more began singing, and the song and the singer faded away together around a bend in the river.

There goes a man who is happy because he is an Indian, thought South Boy. An Indian was not faced with distressing alternatives, nor troubled by thoughts that raged in the back of his mind.

All at once the heat became unbearable. South Boy slid

out of the fork of the tree, down the bank, and into the cool water. He washed the caked mud from his head and ran his fingers through his half-long hair. Then he remembered what old Hook-a-row had said about twisting it into fifty strands and becoming a Real Person.

South Boy rested his head on the root of the willow that projected just above the water and listened to the river grumbling like a drunken old man. It was talking Mojave:

Kee-glug—glug—emk, it said, *go—go*, with a gurgle in the middle of the word.

A great uprooted cottonwood tree came slowly tumbling through the current, end over end, top up first, leaf-covered branches held skyward for a moment, slowly falling over, disappearing beneath the water; then its torn and straggling roots came up to the sun, and down again.

It made South Boy feel sad. Yet his troubles were fading out of his mind, and before he realized it, he was asleep.

CHAPTER II

THE HAWKS

THE WILLOW's shadow on the water was almost gone. The river was higher. It covered South Boy's chest, and a wavelet lapped over his chin and filled his half-open mouth. South Boy sat up straight, sputtering, angry, surprised to see that the sun rode low over the stark, naked ridge on the Nevada side where Beale's Trail crossed like a thin white scar.

The river's voice was louder, still talking—in garbled Mojave.

Then another voice using good, plain Mojave spoke from above and behind, "I saw a dream on your face."

South Boy choked and looked up quickly to see Havek staring down at him from the willow's fork. Then he smiled and spat out river water. Here was company. Here was the end of boredom and worry.

"What did you dream?" Havek insisted. His black eyes were intent and his lips parted. He was a big boy, almost six feet tall —nearly "the size of a man," as the Mojaves say. Being still under the jurisdiction of the government school at the Fort, he wore faded blue jeans and a hickory shirt, and his thick hair was shingled. But being on a vacation at that season of the year his neck was wrapped with perhaps a thousand strands of small blue and white beads, making a very uncomfortable-looking bundle. Across his lap were a six-foot bow and seven hunting arrows, such as any Mojave boy would carry, whether he was in school or not.

South Boy studied for a moment, trying to remember his dream. While it was no matter to him he wanted to oblige Havek, for he knew the great importance Mojaves attached to dreaming; but the dream, when he remembered, seemed such a trivial thing he didn't want to talk about it. Finally he said: "It was nothing. White people always dream nonsense."

"No," said Havek promptly. "Your ghost saw something important. I saw it on your face!" He was leaning far out from the tree, staring almost directly down at South Boy. The flesh on his brown chin quivered so that its two vertical lines of blue tattooing wriggled like little snakes.

"Just dreamed of two hawks, and nothing more," said South Boy.

Havek came down out of the tree as though a bee had stung him. Standing on the bank, clutching his bow and arrows in his left hand, he wiped the sweat from his face with his right sleeve. "Truly!" he whispered. "He's told me truly!"

By this time South Boy began to share some of Havek's excitement. He searched his mind and could not remember anybody ever having told him about the importance of hawk-dreaming. He clambered out of the water and stood dripping on the bank, diffident about showing too much interest for fear Havek might be making game of him. He knew it was a Mojave trick to make a great to-do about some small matter and then break out laughing when the victim began to take it all seriously. Still, Havek wasn't much of a joker.

South Boy picked up his shirt and overalls and doused them in the river to wash away the dried mud. He got into his clothes, shivering a little. The air was little cooler than when he had come to the river; but a strong gusty wind was blowing, and working the same magic on his wet clothes as it did on the water jar.

Finally he said, "What does a hawk-dream mean?"

Havek spoke out of a deep study. "I'm not certain. Complete knowledge in such matters was not given to me. You are white, so it may mean nothing. We must go ask some old man."

Well, South Boy decided, he's certainly in earnest about it.

Then he said, "I saw Hook-a-row going down-river this morning. We can trail him. He won't go far."

Havek shook his head. "My trail goes north. In the north there's a very great *hota* holding a boys' sing beyond the Fort. Can you go there? It is important." He spoke in greatest earnest.

"Well," said South Boy, "that's better than sitting here like a toad on a lump of mud. Let's go."

"But you may not be coming back directly. Fetch something. Be prepared to be gone some days."

"Good!" said South Boy. "There'll be four days of this crazy weather and nothing to do. I'll go home and get my shotgun." And he started off toward the ranch.

"Leave the gun. Bring a bow," Havek called after him.

"I broke my bow," said South Boy.

"Leave the gun, anyway," said Havek. "It's too heavy for traveling."

Thus to escape boredom, with no idea as yet of escaping the horns of his dilemma, South Boy set out on his fateful journey. When he got to the ranch he heard noises that told him the cook was again in the summer kitchen; so he stuck his head inside the screen door and told her he was going visiting and would be gone two or three nights. The cook began thanking the Virgin and the twelve apostles, naming them one by one.

South Boy went to the house and crawled under the back gallery to the hole where the cat had her kittens. From it he took a fishing line with several hooks attached, wrapped around a stick. Then he began to dig in the soft dirt at the bottom of the hole, which was temporarily free of kittens. Three or four inches down he uncovered a bundle carefully wrapped in a greasy rag. He unwrapped the rag and there, well-swathed in axle grease, was a new nickel-plated revolver . . . a weapon that was very dear to him because it was forbidden.

Six months ago he had sent his life's savings to a Chicago

mail-order house and in due course this treasure had been sent to him. No one knew about it, not even Havek. He broke the gun to see that it was loaded, a needless procedure because he knew he hadn't used the last six cartridges he had left in the cylinder a couple of weeks before. He snapped it shut, tucked it under his belt inside his shirt, and backed out into the yard.

Almost as an afterthought he went into the kitchen, took one small box of soda crackers from a shelf and three or four handfuls of black, salty strips of jerky from the meat bin. One of these he crammed into his mouth, sucking gratefully at the salt which his body craved after much sweating.

Thus with a fishline, a box of crackers, a half pound of jerky, an old broken pocketknife, a little water-tight case full of sulphur matches (two items he was never without), and a belly-gun (the latter only a sort of talisman) South Boy felt himself equipped to go anywhere the Colorado flowed.

His clothes were dry now, so that he found the return trip to the river very hot; but he was buoyed up by the prospect of spending the night at the "sing," and by the tantalizing mystery of the hawk-dreaming.

Why was Havek so excited about it?

There was more excitement when he got to the river. He went down into the water to his knees, stooped to drink his fill, slopped water over his head till his half-long hair was dripping-wet, and climbed the bank.

There stood Havek, leaning on his long bow. The seven hunting arrows were thrust into the back of his belt, and in his right hand he held a three-foot willow rod a little thicker than a man's thumb. Bound to this were four carefully fletched arrows. Unlike the hunting arrows, unlike any ordinary Mojave arrows, these had iron points—small, longish, triangular, and quite sharp.

"Apache arrows!" cried South Boy. He had never seen the like twice in his life.

"There's a war," said Havek.

"You go making war with those arrows and the agency police will jug you!" South Boy warned.

"Far," said Havek, jerking his chin toward the north. "Faraway war!"

Then South Boy remembered he had twice heard mention of Piutes that day and he opened his mouth to ask Havek for talk, but Havek was already trotting away along the river bank.

The sun was very low. The trees made much shade. Even when they had turned inland and had passed through the willows and the cottonwoods and were shuffling through the gourd vines in the wide spaces between the mesquite trees, there was still shade. And the wind continued to blow, making the heat bearable. They traveled at a little trot, like roaming dogs.

Suddenly South Boy found himself very content and very comfortable. There was meat and water in his belly and there was salt in his mouth, for he was chewing another strip of jerky. The thoughts that came from the back of his head to worry him were gone entirely. He was a different person. He was his old self. He cared nothing for the future at all—not even for the answer to such tantalizing questions as "Why Apache arrows?" and "What means a hawk-dream?" He just felt good.

He began chuckling to himself as he jogged along. Havek heard him and turned around, saw him chewing and reached back his hand. South Boy reached into his shirt and brought out a great handful of jerky which he thrust into Havek's hand.

When the rim of the sun sat down on the white scar where Beale's Trail crossed the ridge of the Dead Mountains over in Nevada, they came to a place called Ahavelpah where the river bottom ended at the mesa's cliff. Nobody lived there. There had been a rancheria there at one time, but someone had died and been cremated there, and his house and goods burned, of course; so it was a ghost place and would remain so for a generation—just a damp swale near the foot of the dun cliff where three big cottonwoods grew by a water hole.

At the third cottonwood, Havek said, "Wait here," and he climbed the face of the cliff and under the low branches of a mesquite that clung to it ten feet up. Directly, he came sliding down the gravelly face of the mesa carrying a five-pound salt bag bulging full.

"Traveler's rations," he said, stuffing the bag into his shirt.

Then South Boy knew for certain Havek was intending to travel far, for no one would bother carrying a bag of parched corn and pumpkin seeds if he were only going as far as the northern valley, just above the Fort.

This he thought little of at the time. He was more impressed with the fact that Havek had disclosed the location of his secret cache. That was usually concealed from one's closest friend, for it was a great honor to keep something cleverly concealed. South Boy hugged the gun against his belly and laughed to himself. He would show that to Havek some time and tell him triumphantly, "All this time I was traveling with you and you didn't know I had it."

That would be a triumph indeed. Almost a Great Thing.

They were jogging along at the foot of the cliff over ground made hard by the black alkali. Havek began to sing:

"Name-traveling, I travel,
Name-finding, a new name."

So he goes traveling with Apache arrows, thought South Boy. Well . . .

It was likewise unusual for a Mojave boy to go traveling to find himself a man's name before he was through school, that is if he went to school. Havek was setting out a year or two early. Havek hated his boy's name, which was really a baby name. Because it was a joke name, it had stayed with him in his youth. It was such a good joke name that he was called Havek even by people who habitually spoke English and should have called him by his government name, which was Rutherford Hayes.

The joke was Havek's mother's. She was a huge woman, always laughing. When she carried Havek, she grew so large she thought she was going to have twins. When Havek came alone, she laughed and laughed, and called him *Havek*, which means simply "Two."

Soon they came to a wide mouth of a wash, and Havek turned up the sandy bed of the arroyo that came out of it. He slowed his pace down to a walk, for the bed was sand and the going was heavy.

South Boy stopped once to look back over his shoulder. The sun was gone, and the west was as red as a shirt of China silk. A lovely thing to see.

This, he told himself, I'll remember a long time. This is the night I was happy, after a bad day.

He thought of something he heard an old man say: "The white man's forehead is wrinkled because he is always asking, 'Will tomorrow be bad?' He never has time to smile because it is very good right now."

It is very good right now, thought South Boy. I'll let tomorrow be.

Up ahead Havek trudged on past a paloverde tree, green of trunk, branch, and stem, and very beautiful against the white sand of the wash. He was going slower because the sand pulled at his heels. He passed the first greasewood bush—a dozen gray-green stems springing out of a common center and tipped with twigs bearing tiny, crinkly, greasy-green leaves.

On past was one smoke tree with a ghostly crown of innumerable gray, leafless twigs, and when Havek reached the smoke tree, the first bat of the evening came circling over his head. Havek immediately swallowed the meat he was chewing on and began to sing:

> "Over our house
> The night bat
> Rising, flies . . ."

That was the first song in the long dream-singing called "The Ravens."

Now there is something to think about, said South Boy to himself. This business of dream-singing.

About two years before, Havek had begun singing "The Ravens." When South Boy asked him how he learned it Havek said: "I dreamed it. It was given to me, just so, because my shadow stood outside the Sacred House and heard the Ravens singing. I was unborn, but I was there. So now I have dreamed what I heard and saw."

That's tougher to understand than Christian Instruction, thought South Boy. It didn't seem likely to him that anybody could go to sleep and dream two hundred songs in their proper meter and rhythm, not to mention complicated melody and long meandering story—for the songs only gave outline and emphasis to the tale.

"How can he dream all that when it takes him two nights to sing and tell all of it?"

In camp Havek would intersperse his tale between his songs. Now he just sang. About two semi-embodied spirits who woke up in the Sacred House. They heard bats squeaking overhead, so they sang about bats. Then, being children, they reached for their toys. So Havek sang:

"We reach,
And there is a rattle
In each hand . . ."

So sang the spirits as they danced towards the door of the Sacred House, and so Havek sang as he trudged up the arroyo to the mesa top—about rattles and cane buzzers, and what the world would look like when it was completed.

When they reached the door, the Ravens looked out across the valley of the Colorado where the Mojaves, yet to be created, were going to live. They saw something out of the future: the dust of a war party returning from a successful raid to the east, over in the Apache country. Painted men, mallet-headed clubs dangling from their wrists by leather thongs, bound slaves, the whole skin of a man's head waving like a flag atop a tall pole, the dance of triumph and the smoking of those made unclean by blood and death.

Havek sang on as he came out of the wash and turned due north across the flat top of the mesa where traveling was good over a matrix of fine firm gravel. He broke into a trot. Up here the little greasewood bushes grew in even spacings, twelve yards apart and no more than three feet high. Nothing else grew here but an occasional cholla cactus.

South Boy was saying to himself: "His grandfather sang 'The Ravens.' Havek may have dreamed it, but I'll bet he learned it from the old man first."

The moon came up over Arizona mountains, fifteen miles across the mesa—very red, very large, very bright. The little greasewoods cast long, pale, spindling shadows towards the now distant river. The breeze began blowing stronger. It was still hot, but the breeze made it pleasant.

Havek's song grew a little monotonous. The Raven brothers went name-traveling after they left the Sacred House. Havek's song became an unending recital of the names of mountains, canyons, springs, and streams that they saw as they wandered west to the San Bernardino Mountains where they looked upon the distant sea, then south and east to the mouth of the Colorado and east and north through Pima and Apache country.

An easy way to get your geography, if you could dream all that. Suppose I could go to sleep and dream the whole of Tarr and McMurry's . . . South Boy was thinking when he saw the lights of Fort Mojave over to the left, where the mesa pushed a projecting peninsula right down to the river.

The Fort looked like a city to South Boy, with its dozen big buildings, two of them monsters—two stories high. There were very few lights tonight. He had seen it one night last winter, when school was in session—lights blazing from every window. A stupendous sight. Breath-taking. Counting the In-

dian children there were three hundred people in those buildings! Even now when there was only maintenance staff and a
half-dozen lighted windows, the sight of the Fort was thrilling
enough to make him forget the glory of the night and his hap-
hazard speculations on dream singing.

A little farther north was a row of three lights close together—the trader's store. From there came the faint screech
of a phonograph playing that new song "Redwing." He was
too far away to see, but he knew the phonograph would be on
a cracker box just outside the door. Young Mojaves would be
perched in a long row on the hitching rail; old people, sitting
on the ground; a white man or two from the Fort; maybe even
a white lady sitting in the trader's rocking chair.

Havek stopped singing to listen. South Boy wished he would
turn aside, but he went trotting on.

Suddenly the phonograph was drowned out by a chorus of
strong voices.

> "Oh the moon shines bright on pretty Redwing,
> The breezes sighing, the night bird crying,
> For far beneath his star her brave is sleeping,
> While Redwing's weeping
> Her heart away."

Havek threw back his head and joined in with the distant
singers. Nothing could be more different from the Raven singing than this tin-pan-alley product. But Havek proved the saying, "A Mojave can sing anything."

South Boy just listened with throbbing pleasure and a little
melancholy, partly because of the sad plight of Redwing and
partly because he had long since learned he could not sing.

The song faded, the lights grew dim and mingled with the
lower stars. Before long they came to the place where the mesa
dropped off again. Below them the mesquite floor stretched
north as far as their eyes could see. Here and there were barren,
alkali-encrusted playas that shone pale silver in the moonlight.
A narrow, snaky lagoon began a mile away and wiggled off

into the distance, its gray water showing a darker silver. There
was a faint flicker of fire at the near end of it.

By that fire the hota would be holding the sing.

Havek stopped and leaned on his bow. South Boy stopped
and looked at him expectantly.

Havek spat into the dark shadow that fringed the foot of
the cliff.

"Nebethee's down there, if he came up-river tonight."

"Uh-huh," said South Boy, speculatively. He walked to
the very edge of the cliff and spat reflectively into the void,
peering into the depth of the shadow, not anxiously, but with
a certain sharp interest.

"Nebethee caught Pahto-shali-la and ate him, bones and all,
and Pahto-shali-la was a full-sized man and a good fighter."

South Boy could have given Havek an argument on that.
White people maintained that the Mojave got drunk and fell
into the river at flood time. But South Boy's mind was too busy
for arguments. He was swiftly reviewing the Mormonhater's
ideas on the cannibalistic monster that the white people called
the "Mojaves' devil."

"Are you afraid to go down here?" asked Havek.

South Boy shook his head. The time had been when he
would have cringed with terror at the mention of Nebethee's
name. When he was very small a big Indian girl had taken him
to the brink of an old well and made him look down into the
dark at their mingled reflections on the water. "Nebethee!"
she said. "He will eat you!" That had scared him into a fit.

He was still too young to know better than to take tales of
Indian doings to his mother—so he ran bellowing to her and
had his first impression of Nebethee pretty well shaken out of
him. Nebethee was just heathen nonsense. It was wicked to be
afraid of him, because he was a heathen lie. By way of comfort
he received the first of several lectures on the *real* or Presbyterian devil. A very different creature, indeed. South Boy had
since acquired a shadowy, uneasy understanding of a complex

of white or Christian devils that had overshadowed Nebethee completely.

But all that was by the way. About two years ago he had discovered by chance that in the dark of the moon the Mormon-hater was doing some very mysterious hunting in the darkest places, and a good deal of it was around the big rock in the river below Needles that the Mojaves called "Nebethee's house." It took a year of chance, infrequent visits with the old trapper to wheedle the reason out of him.

The Mormonhater had many years ago seen a stuffed gorilla in a dime museum in San Francisco, so badly moth-eaten that it was about to fall apart. The proprietor was very sad about its condition. He said he'd give a hundred dollars for a fresh one.

The Mormonhater returned to his boat, his dogs and his trap lines, and in due course he began to give ear to the Mojave stories and descriptions of Nebethee. Then all at once it came to him! Nebethee was nothing else than a great, nocturnal ape. He wrote to the keeper of the dime museum and asked him how much he'd give for such a creature—hide and carcass.

He got a letter back—he even let South Boy read it. There in black and white was the offer of one million dollars for any gorilla shot in the Colorado River valley, plus an invitation for the Mormonhater to head a parade along the whole length of Market Street in an open carriage with the mayor of the city on one side of him, the carcass of the beast on the other.

The Mormonhater had fished his Bible out of his cartridge bag and made South Boy swear, with his right hand on the Book that he'd never tell anyone.

South Boy went home and carefully read everything that the Advanced Geography had to say about the great apes, and studied the very inadequate picture shown in it.

He hadn't promised not to hunt the creature himself.

However, Nebethee-hunting had proven very poor around the ranch. Up here, down in that shadow, might be his golden opportunity.

A million dollars . . . that was all the money in the world. He'd give the Mormonhater half. He'd even let the Mormonhater share the carriage with him and the mayor and the late Nebethee.

Of course the geography said that gorillas were only found in Africa, and that they were herbivorous. But the geography said nothing at all about Mojaves or the Colorado River valley. It showed complete ignorance about this part of the world.

So South Boy stared eagerly into the cliff's shadow and started off in a trot along its rim, looking for a place to descend. While the idea of crowds of strange people gave him shudders under most conditions, the thought of that crowd along Market Street in San Francisco made him feel good. Maybe it was because they would be cheering him. That's what the Mormonhater said: "They'll be yelling their heads off!"

Not far away he found a slide: a place where the smaller boys from the Fort came on Saturdays to slide down the steep, gravelly face of the mesa on boards—the equivalent of tobagganing in a snowless country. He could go down there without getting his pants full of prickly pear and cholla.

So he paused at the top of the slide and called to Havek: "Tell me, have I heard truly? Does Nebethee look like a big, thick, hairy man that's hunchbacked and stooped over?"

"Truly! Truly!" said Havek, his breath whistling in his excitement.

A million dollars and a parade! thought South Boy as he disappeared into the black on a minor avalanche of gravel.

His hand was inside his shirt, gripping the butt of his shortgun. He had a feeling he'd be better satisfied if he had a weapon of heavier caliber—one that he'd tried out on something more than tin cans at very short range. Still, this would be close-range work. He'd let Nebethee come twice arm-length and he'd put six bullets into his belly. After all, an ape was just a big, tough, hairy man. All the experts agreed—and there was hardly a man in the Valley but was at least a theoretical expert on homicide—that a bullet in the belly was the sure way of stopping a real tough man. The Foreman said (and it was well known he was more than a theoretical expert), "A bullet in the belly button beats two through the head."

The gravel stopped rolling under the seat of South Boy's pants and his feet hit soft dirt and hit running. He ran only as far as the first mesquite and there he crouched, his back protected by the thorny tree. He found he could see surprisingly well. There was nothing but low soap-weeds for yards around him. No hiding place for anything bigger than a rabbit. His heart beat hard, his imagination sent false, fleeting images to his eyes, but as a veteran of many a night hunt he knew he saw nothing real.

His heart eased and sank in slow, leaden disappointment.

He might have been there two minutes when he heard Havek's yell. The yell of a warrior who goes to look into the face of death. Havek was coming down the gravel slide, invisible, but audible.

Havek came running across the flat, a swiftly moving blackness in a world less black. Nothing else moved. South Boy, hope fading, got up and trotted after him, still crouching low, his hand on his belly-gun. Havek was out in the moonlight, and he stopped in a small white playa.

"South Boy!" he called anxiously. "South Boy!"

South Boy came walking out of the shadows, slowly. Somehow he'd been so sure of a million dollars and glory a minute ago. Now he had a sickening feeling.

That Mormonhater was crazy! Everyone said so. South Boy didn't want to believe it. The Mormonhater was his friend. But if Nebethee were an ape, there would have to be more than one. Apes have to breed and die like other creatures. Why hadn't he thought of that before working his hopes up so high?

He came up to where Havek stood, and walked by him in glum silence.

Havek was staring at him, his mouth open, the whites of

his eyes showing. "Truly," he muttered. "Truly. A hawk-dreamer. His hands empty. He went down into Death's face. He walked slowly away. Truly—truly—truly—a Great Thing."

South Boy heard him and felt low and cheap. Havek thought he had done a brave thing. Instead he'd just made a fool of himself, believing a crazy man's story. He could not explain because he had promised the Mormonhater. And how could he explain a thing like that to an Indian, anyway?

So he walked in silence, which was exactly what a Mojave would have done after an act of great courage. Havek followed him, murmuring delightedly; and South Boy felt all the more like a cheat, and his heart was lower than a snake's belly.

The trouble is, he was thinking, I act Indian one time and white another time and I get all mixed. He tried to think that idea out to make it more coherent, but he couldn't.

Chapter III

THE DREAM SINGERS

The place of the singing was called Wahl-Khi-Walka, according to Havek. It was an old clearing so full of both black and white alkali that it remained fairly free of brush and weeds except for an occasional mesquite that grew on the bank of the Snake lagoon. Someone had built there a ramada, or a "shade," or a willow-roof, as it was variously called: a brush thatch supported by six posts. It was crudely made and plainly no one lived there permanently.

The singer and his audience were not under the ramada, but seated out in the open in a wide circle around a fire that was made small to give out the greatest light with the least possible heat. The first person South Boy saw was the fire tender, a boy two or three years younger than himself. He was standing —the fire throwing glistening high lights on his naked body.

One by one the seated figures began to appear—the hota on the far side of the fire, the light flickering across his painted face. The fire blazed up as the naked boy tossed a dry stick into the flames, bringing the scene out in bright relief. There was a big boy seated on either side of the fire tender, each wearing everyday clothes of the government school—exactly like Havek's. The one between the fire tender and the hota was singing. He was very fat.

Across from these three, that is, on the hota's right, sat two young men, obviously not attending school. Thus there was a wide space to the east of the fire, and there Havek and South Boy sat down, South Boy being careful to sit man-fashion, his knees forward, his legs folded back under his thighs. This was very uncomfortable for him. He was accustomed to crouching

33

on his heels like a white man, or to sit cross-legged like a Yavapai man, or a Mojave child, or a woman.

South Boy's first interest was in the hota. Looking across the fire with politely veiled curiosity, he saw a man perhaps fifty years old, very tall, heavy of shoulders and body, serious and calm of face, his long hair newly dressed and glossy black and twisted into thirty or forty little ropes tied together at the nape of his neck and hanging down his back. There was a band of red paint straight across his face, from just under his eyes to his upper lip, that was broken in the middle by a narrow yellow stripe running the length of his nose. He wore white man's pants and a cotton undershirt.

He nodded when the two sat down, and looked surprised to see South Boy.

South Boy turned his eyes to the singer, who at that moment ceased singing and took up the narrative—about two Cat Brothers, Lion and Jaguar, as they traveled from the Virgin River in Utah, down into Mexico. South Boy concluded that the fat boy had dreamed for himself a very dreary singing. It was a geography lesson at its worst—a fabulously complete recital of place names filled with wearisome data on exactly what the heroes thought and said and ate at each place, the animals they saw, how they made bows and arrows and suchlike.

At the rate the fat boy was going, it would be morning before he got the Cats down-river as far as Parker, even.

This side of the fat boy, the naked fire tender listened intently. Plainly, a bush boy who had never been to school. His hair was a tousled mop, and his face bore fresh tattoo marks. Every now and then he carefully placed a small, dry stick on the fire to keep it blazing. But he was listening all the time. South Boy began to wonder whether this boy would claim in later years that he had dreamed this Cat singing, and how much of it he would actually dream and how much he would have learned while fire-tending.

Next to the little boy—between him and Havek—was another big schoolboy, an anonymous lout whom South Boy knew without knowing much about him.

Those on the south side were very different. The first, nearest to South Boy, wore the half-long hair of mourning, and a very dirty suit of white man's clothes. He had a long-healed scrofulous sore on the side of his neck and there was a wild, fanatical gleam in his eyes. He was full-grown, possibly sixteen, and it was obvious from both his appearance and his physical condition that he had never been to school.

Beyond him, nearest to the hota, was a very tall young man, six feet three or four, perhaps eighteen or nineteen. Probably a school graduate. Now he was a perfect Mojave dandy, according to the fashion of his generation. He wore his hair long and rope-twisted, newly dressed and glossy like the hota's, but the young man had an eagle feather tied to his after-lock by a foot of gut-string, and it fell forward—its vermilion-dyed tip resting just in front of his left shoulder. He wore a shirt of salmon-colored China silk—very popular then—so thin that even in the firelight the glint of his sweaty-brown skin showed through it. On his arms were green sleeve garters, and to each one were tied foot-long streamers of inch-wide ribbon in several colors—ornaments that were called "catch-the-girls." There was a weary, surfeited, and even haunted expression on his handsome, good-natured face. All South Boy knew about that was implied in the fact that this young man's chosen name was "Come-into-the-Brush," and that he had seen much the same look on the face of a Needles gambler around whom the saloon biddies flocked like buzzards around a dead cow.

The hota sat still for a while. The fat boy changed again from narrative to song, and his songs were the more dreary because they were set in a stilted language, distorted to fit the meter. South Boy couldn't understand it.

The hota got up, walked away a few steps, and stood looking down at the ground. Havek immediately got up and walked around the group and began talking to the hota, almost whispering—but very rapidly. South Boy noticed that Havek had walked slightly stiff in the right leg. His bow and hunting arrows lay where he had been sitting, but the bundle of war arrows were not there. Havek must have thrust them down his pants leg.

The singing grew jerky and uncertain, and finally ended in a sulky grunt. Nobody was listening now, not even the fire tender. Everybody watched the hota and Havek, except the singer, who glared venomously at South Boy—for it was very obvious that he was the cause of the interruption.

By and by the hota walked back to his place and Havek came around the fire and sat down in his place. His face was blank, as though nothing had occurred. He whispered, "In the morning," without looking around.

That's right, thought South Boy. The hota will dream before he gives an answer.

South Boy looked up at the low-hanging stars and said to himself: "I won't wrinkle my forehead over what he might say in the morning. I'll enjoy what is right now, like an Indian." Right now was very pleasant. The breeze came quite steadily to fan his face as he picked out a triangle of stars, a bright one in the apex and two lesser ones below. They would be his clock to gauge the passing of the night. A bull bat soared across his stars. There was an owl hunting somewhere on silent wings, twittering and chuckling to herself. Across the lagoon a coyote went *Yep-yip-yip-yeow-ow!* Pack rats rustled in the weeds, and a thousand distant insects made a faint, persistent background of sound.

Suddenly the night noises were silenced by a staccato burst of words. The boy with the scarred neck was on his feet orating in short, jerky, stylized phrases—in a manner called by English-speaking Mojaves "funeral preaching." He had the strong voice and the dynamic, whole-souled delivery of a back-country evangelist. South Boy had heard the like only once—under an old rag of a tent down in Phoenix, where a pale young man preached and white men and white women yelled and prayed as if they were crazy and even beat their heads against the rough planks of the preacher's platform.

The wild boy "preached" the world's beginning. In his dream he had been given the memory of what his shadow had seen in the First Times. Small, naked, and frightened, he had been there in a nebulous crowd of unformed beings when Earth and Sky touched on the far side of the Western Ocean, and Mutavilya, the First God, was born out of the resulting cataclysm.

Then Mutavilya gathered together the shadows, space-wanderers until that time, and carried them across the ocean to Avapoolpo near where, in time to come, the Colorado would flow by in El Dorado Canyon. Here he built the Sacred House of logs and thatched it with arrowweeds and covered it over with sand—setting the pattern for every Mojave's winter house for all time to come.

Scar-Neck built the house for his audience log by log, naming them all and placing them in position. When the house was finished he stood by the door while Mutavilya and certain shadows went inside. He heard the First God teach them the formulas that gave them the accursed power of life and death, for those within would dream these formulas after they were born and become "doctors," feared by the people.

He saw the first full-powered doctor come out of the dark doorway. She was Haynee (Frog), Mutavilya's daughter. He saw murder in her face and he tried to cry out and warn Mutavilya—but he was a shadow and had no voice.

He witnessed the filthy practices by which Haynee made the God sick and saw the sweat of agony on Mutavilya's face when he stepped out into the light.

So Mutavilya announced the approach of the First Death, and he called his son, Mastamho, to him and before all the unborn souls he gave instructions for the First Cremation.

Sweat and tears streaked the boy's dirty face and his words

burst forth in a choking stream as he told how the fire hole was dug and logs laid down, and how the cry of the loon arose at the moment of death, and the body was laid on the pyre, and the logs piled over it.

South Boy looked around. Everybody was crying.

So the God had died and had been laid on the burning pile, and thus every man died and was so laid, and the cry of the loon sang out from human throats in the tumult of grief each time death came.

South Boy brushed away his own tears with the back of his hand. He hated this part of the story. The Indians could cry out their grief and be done with it. He couldn't. He'd tried it before.

With infinite detail Scar-Neck told how there was yet no fire and Coyote was sent to beg fire from the Farther Mountains, and how he stole the Egg of Fire without asking, thus branding himself as a thief for all time. A woman called Fly rubbed the cold Fire embryo on her leg until it heated and burst and she threw it on the cremation pile and the flames leaped up.

The mourners formed their circle. Everyone wailed aloud but White Man. His cold, white face was like a rock. He knew he didn't belong there; so he sank into the ground with a noise like a cannon shot and, traveling underground and under the sea, he returned to Asia, the place of primal origin. When he returned centuries later, he brought back with him the roar of the cannon.

South Boy saw Havek and two or three others look at him at this point of the story, but he was crying like the others now so that he didn't feel conspicuous. Maybe this time he could cry hard and feel better afterwards.

The story went into a seeming purposeless digression. Coyote had been refused a place in the mourning circle because he was a thief. So he went trotting around it, after the manner of all curious coyotes from that time on. Badger was the short man in the circle and his head was bowed low as he wept. When the heat burst the body, Coyote leaped over Badger's head, seized the God's heart and ran away with it. So Coyote became very wise, but every man's hand is against him.

Thus Mutavilya became a heap of indestructible ashes. But, as any remainder of the dead is always an offense, Mastamho tried to get rid of them. He made rain and hail, but the ashes remained. Then Mastamho made the Colorado to wash away the ashes of his father . . .

South Boy looked up at the sky. His triangle of stars was half down toward the Nevada mountains, and the moon rode in the top of the sky. This would be an all-night telling.

. . . Mastamho went up to the high Rockies, and there he broke the Egg of Waters with a stick of breath and saliva, and on a tule raft he rode the flood, breaking through the mountains, cutting the great gash called the Grand Canyon, cutting Boulder and Black Canyons, cutting El Dorado Canyon, and washing the ashes away before him.

"I was there," chanted Scar-Neck with staccato eagerness. "I rode the raft with Mastamho. Below Hardyville he said, 'I'll make wide bottom land,' and he threw the raft from side to side, spreading the water. Then he was tired. He stood still. The water cut the canyon below Needles. And so on down he made bottom land and canyons until the water spread ahead of him and made the great flat between Yuma and the sea . . ."

South Boy was thinking of the time he went down-river in the height of the big flood, booming through eight-foot sand rollers in a flat-bottom boat, smashing through each brown crest, crashing with a spine-tingling jolt into every through trough—and the memory of it made the story of the river's making very real to him.

He looked again at the sky and saw that the moon was a quarter down to the west. Still the scar-necked boy preached on without evidence of tiring. He was telling how the raft landed on a mountain down in the Yaqui country in Mexico.

There Mastamho looked far to the south and saw the Sky Rattlesnake who ruled the Mexicans in their mountain valley. He didn't want his people to have such a dangerous neighbor, so he began gathering them up in his arms to take them up-river again. But some said, "We stay!" So he gave them bodies of men and they became Yaquis, and they live there and fight Mexicans to this day.

At this point the naked fire tender curled up in his place to sleep. So South Boy lay down and stretched out his cramped legs.

The story was no longer dramatic. It became an endless description of how Mastamho came up the valley of the Colorado, stopping here and there to give bodies to various groups of people, and to send them away with full instructions as to what manner of life they should follow in the future.

South Boy napped. He missed much of the telling, but he'd heard the rest at several cremations: how Mastamho gave the last and biggest bodies to the Mojaves and taught them to make pottery and plant crops, and how to travel and make war . . .

The triangle of stars was long gone, and the moon was low. Scar-Neck was still preaching. South Boy opened his eyes. Havek and the fat boy were asleep. The fire tender was up. The man called Come-into-the-Brush sat with his chin on his chest and the eagle feather dangling across his face. The rest were awake, listening.

. . . Mastamho had lured Sky Rattlesnake into Mojave country and killed him. His long body went writhing back down-river to Mexico. His blood splattered. From it sprang lice, and singing ants, then as the blood clots grew bigger came spiders, scorpions, centipedes, Gila monsters, little and big rattlesnakes, then alligators.

When Mastamho had done his work, he was weary. He stood on a high place, stretched out his arms and straightway lost his divinity. He become a stinking fish hawk, covered with vermin, but devoid of memory and oblivious of all care. So he flew away, leaving creation strictly on its own.

Just before he went back to sleep, South Boy thought: That is why Mojaves never pray—they have no God left to pray to.

Chapter IV

RUNAWAY

When South Boy again awoke he opened his eyes on the half-light of first dawn. The sky was graying out over the black, ragged rim of the Arizona mountains. He got up, stretched himself, and walked slowly through the circle of sprawled sleeping forms, across the dead fire, down to the lagoon. Ahead was a scraggly mesquite about fifteen feet high, its top branches killed by the mistletoe that clung like a huge, untidy magpie's nest to its topmost fork. A buck quail sat atop the mistletoe looking down at South Boy, his little head feather drooping rakishly over his left eye. He called out in a sleepy voice, "Go-back-home! Go-back-home!" His words were English, and plain as anything.

South Boy picked up a stick and threw it at him. If that was an omen, he wasn't going to say anything about it. Then he caught sight of an old rag half covered with silt and lacy mesquite leaves. Immediately his mind registered, Scorpion! and he bristled with the pious feud he unendingly carried out against all the brood that sprang from Sky Rattlesnake's blood.

Eagerly he flipped the rag aside. There she was—three inches long, yellow and black, her many-jointed, sting-tipped tail curved over her back, and miniature crayfish claws stretched out menacingly. South Boy flipped the rag back over her and stamped down hard with his bare, horn-calloused heel. He flipped the rag aside again. She was plenty dead.

The bank of the lagoon dropped off five feet into gray water. South Boy wriggled out of his clothes, hid the gun and box of crackers under his shirt and jumped in. The water was as warm as soup—not at all like the bracing, swift, soil-red water of the river. South Boy washed the sweat out of his hair and climbed out on the bank.

That moment the hota and Havek came down past the mesquite tree. Havek was naked, and the hota was stripped down to a G string. Both spoke to South Boy. Havek jumped out into the lagoon, the hota stepped over the bank as though it were no higher than a stair tread, and, knee-deep in the water, began washing the paint from his face. When he was through, he said, "This, then is the hawk-dreamer?"

"I dreamed thus," assented South Boy.

"Truly! Truly!" cried Havek. He was floating on his back about ten yards out. "I saw the dream on his face."

By and by the hota asked, "Who taught you to speak Mojave?"

South Boy stared at him blankly. "Nobody," he said.

Havek put in. "He was born down-river. So they call him South Boy. I think a woman of the Hupa clan nursed him."

"Truly," said South Boy.

"Yes, I remember now. Most things about white people I do not know," said the hota proudly. "I am of the people who cling to the old ways." He stood still for some time looking over the water. At last he said: "There is no use denying it. Milk becomes flesh and blood. In so much, then, you are a Proper Person. So as you dream, thus you are. No doubt you will travel bravely the trail north." Then he began "preaching."

"The white man's son. I won't advise him. I won't know where he goes. There'll be trouble. Anger down-river. Cowboys looking. Reservation police looking. Up-river, there's trouble. Piutes killed somebody. A white man, surely. Through enemy country. A hawk flies.

"In enemy country, wisdom is caution. Night is a friend. Darkness blinds bullets. Horses cannot run over rocks. Bullets can't see through thick brush!"

Then he jumped up onto the bank—a feat of strength and

agility that almost took South Boy's breath away. "I know because I dreamed—a great thing will be done!" he said, and stalked back to camp.

"See, I told you!" said Havek.

"You told me what? Nobody told me nothing! What's it all about?" replied South Boy.

"He says you're a sure enough hawk-dreamer, and you'll do a Great Thing in the Piute country."

South Boy was silent for a moment. Then he said in English: "Well, tie me down! I didn't figger on going so far!"

"You, being white, see blindly. When I dreamed of hawks I knew. A brave man dreams of hawks just before a war. My hawk-dream came night before last, and, sure enough, yesterday came word that there was war among the Piutes. So I took my arrows and started north, and directly I found you sleeping with a dream upon your face."

At the moment South Boy felt like a man who had fallen into a river in flood time—that he was being carried he knew not where by currents he could neither breast nor control. He didn't know whether he should be elated or frightened. He stood with his mouth open, trying to think.

Just then he looked behind him and saw all the rest of the boys who had attended last night's singing come trooping down from the direction of the willow-roof. They came silently, staring at South Boy. They were all in a bunch except for the fat boy who had been singing "The Cats" when Havek and South Boy arrived. He was stalking along five paces ahead of the pack, with a sullen face and blood in his eye.

This was the common Mojave approach when starting a fight—a bold, sullen advance, backed by friends who do not come as participants, but as witnesses and counselors. Havek promptly got out of the water and stood five paces to one side of South Boy. The hota folded his arms and stood farther away to the other side.

South Boy had a momentary queasy feeling, for the fat boy

was nearly a head taller and outweighed him fifty pounds. But the fat boy was very fat, and he had on clothes. South Boy was lean, naked, wet, and slippery.

Some twenty paces away the fat boy stopped and said, "Half-long-hair. Your mother is dead."

Whether South Boy's mother was dead or not, this was the foulest of insults. It was so vile it was surprising, for it was seldom used by sober men or big boys, only by drunken or angry women, and dirty-mouthed youngsters. The fat boy was evidently very angry indeed over the way the arrival of Havek and South Boy had spoiled his "sing."

The fact that South Boy was too surprised to reply immediately with invectives of his own was mistaken by the hostile witnesses as an indication of fear. The little fire tender, the dirty, scar-necked boy, and the big sullen schoolboy set up a chorus of cackling jeers as the fat boy advanced. Scar-Neck was particularly vicious. He seemed to take a sadist's joy in humiliating the vanquished.

South Boy's eyes were on his opponent's big body. His face flushed brick-colored. He began naming over all the terms of relationship he knew in Mojave, added some in English and a few in Mexican. Then he cried, "Dead! All dead!"

The blood drained from the fat boy's face. He came on slowly, his hands stretched out, his face bleached a dirty yellow.

South Boy was thinking of certain oft-repeated and well practiced instructions he'd received from the Foreman, a barroom fighter of great distinction. "Let 'em come and butt 'em low." At the distance of two paces South Boy leaped like a frog. It was like butting into a haystack.

The fat boy went down with a mighty "Oomph." South Boy sprang back. A yell went up all around, like the yell at a baseball park when someone hits a home run.

The fat boy sat bug-eyed, all his malice gone. "Where'd you learn that?" he demanded in good school English.

"Our Foreman showed me," said South Boy. "I used to prac-

tice on him, but butting his belly was like butting a board. It's
a good way to down a big man, like he told me."

Everyone was laughing and talking now. The fat boy pulled
from his pocket a new blue bandanna, his only possession of
value. "You teach me, I'll give you this."

South Boy looked thoughtful. "Well, it's going to be hot. Do
my hair up in mud and it's a deal."

So the fat boy went happily to work plastering South Boy's
rope-colored hair with slick underwater mud and tying the
blue handkerchief over it. Five minutes later they found a
bight in the bank with good footing under it, and the fat boy
was crouching, running, butting his head into the crumbly silt
with great vigor and determination.

Such was a fight among the Mojaves. Quick anger and no
malice. South Boy wondered afterwards if this one hadn't been
more or less instigated by the hota to test his courage, for he
came to believe more and more that practical men didn't depend quite so thoroughly on dreams as they let on.

He left the fat boy still butting the bank, found his clothes,
and dressed with great dexterity and seeming carelessness, hiding his gun and the box of crackers until he could conceal them
both beneath his shirt. Of course the crackers made a big bulge;
but that would be taken as a bag of traveler's rations, and no
one would mention it. However, if it were known that South
Boy carried such a luxury as crackers everyone would demand
that he give them to the hota as a present, and the hota would
promptly pass the box around, for a hota never kept anything
for himself.

South Boy was thinking: *If* I'm going to the Piute country
I'll need a particularly good bow and good arrows. I should
get the Whisperer to make them for me, and I'll need this box
of crackers for a present. Not that South Boy couldn't make
a bow of his own, but the Whisperer was an expert.

So he went to the ramada in search of Havek. There he
found him, leaning on his bow, talking to the hota and the ele-

gant young man in the silk shirt. They greeted South Boy with respect and made room for him in the circle as though he were already a grown man.

Havek was saying: "There is no use in Come-into-the-Brush coming with us now. There would be no luck in it. Wait till he dreams right, then he can follow. We won't travel fast right away. He can catch up with us."

"As I said," said the hota.

The young man nodded his head reluctantly.

The hota went to where his clothes lay and brought back a big clasp knife. This he handed to Havek. "You'll need it."

Havek's eyes shone with pleasure, but he said nothing as he pocketed the knife. Then he looked at the bulge in South Boy's shirt; but before he could say anything South Boy said:

"I need a bow and arrows. Let's go the Whisperer's quickly, before it's too hot."

"Good," said the hota. "Tell him to give you a good bow. Tell him I ask it. Good traveling!"

Thus dismissed, South Boy set out along the lagoon at a rapid trot, for the sun had just shone a blazing rim over the ridge and the heat would be mounting rapidly.

So there was war in the north. So that was what the white men in the boat had been talking about, and that was what the Mojave on the log had tried to tell him. And he and Havek, being hawk-dreamers, for destiny and glory were going to travel the far, unknown, all-but-uninhabited Piute country. It would be two hundred miles to the nearest Piute villages, maybe farther.

So they ran on, with South Boy feeling for the first time the heart-lifting elation of glory-to-come. Then a thought struck him. Suppose that the Mormonhater's story were some-how true? Which would be a greater thing—collecting a million dollars for Nebethee's carcass and riding down Market Street with the mayor, or returning in triumph from a journey through a fierce and hostile land to be welcomed in every camp by people singing, to be feasted everywhere, to be called by a magnificent new name?

He mulled this over in his mind for a hundred and six jogging paces while the new sun drew the day's first sweat through his skin. Then he sighed and decided that there was no choice between the two. One was a white man's thing. One was an Indian thing. There was no comparison possible.

They came to an old brush-grown field, and Havek stumbled over a vine. He picked it up and five little white-rinded melons came out of the weeds with it.

Havek said, "We eat," and began kicking through the weeds for more melons.

Without a word South Boy went over to a cottonwood tree that grew immediately on the bank and sat down and started untangling his fishline. Then he searched until he found one last dirty, disreputable sweat-softened piece of jerky in his pocket, baited the three hooks on his line and threw them out into the water. Then he started gathering dry sticks. The fish were biting before he had all his firewood piles and he soon had six little yellow catfish tumbling about on the bank.

These fish were a great mystery to South Boy and to all the Mojaves. Until two years before they had been entirely unknown in the Colorado. Then they suddenly appeared in great numbers. Because they had not been in the creation of the First Times, the older Mojaves thought they were poisonous. South Boy's father found them in the irrigation ditch and ate them with great joy. He said they came from Texas. The Foreman said, "Texas has been getting so dry lately they had to hike a thousand miles overland to find permanent water."

Whatever their origin, they came as a boon to all boys, white or Mojave. For they took bait eagerly—which native fish usually did not, and proved to be the best eating of any fish in the river.

South Boy took his brass match case from the watch pocket of his overalls, opened it and carefully counted the matches.

Sixty-two. He had to make them last. Thus he was for the first time planning for a long journey, and still he wasn't thinking much about it. He spent a match, and the fire was blazing. He gutted the fish with his broken knife, laid them out on a slab of bark near the fire and turned to pull in another one. Havek was coming back, his arms full of little white melons.

Then he heard a drumming of feet coming from the other direction. The gorgeous young man in the silk shirt appeared out of the brush and ran up breathlessly. "Here," he said, and he threw a big knife, like the one the hota had given Havek, down beside South Boy. "Big enough to cut off a head," he gasped. "I haven't dreamed right, so I send my knife. If I dream in four days, I'll follow your trail." He turned and ran back the way he had come.

Havek came and knelt by the fire, letting a dozen little white melons roll out of his arms onto the ground. "That man is sick of the name he took for himself," he said, watching the rapidly retreating silk shirt. "He wants a new one. Maybe it's too late for his dreams to change. I don't know." He fell to raking coals out of the fire with a bit of stick, and when he had a small bed he laid a fish on it to roast.

As for South Boy, he was handling the big knife gingerly as though he were afraid of it, and at the same time he was eyeing it with great pride and admiration. Straightway he took it down to the water, opened the one big blade, washed the whole thing thoroughly, then thrust the blade into the mud, working it rapidly up and down, washed it again, then scoured it with dry sand and a green arrowweed stick, and washed it a third time.

Still he looked at the knife doubtfully. So he climbed the bank, threw a handful of green arrowweed tops into the north side of the fire and passed the knife time and again through the thick smoke.

Havek roasted and ate fish and watched the operation with keen interest. Finally he said, "I never heard of cleaning a knife that way unless you've already cut a man's head off with it."

South Boy shrugged. "There may be a devil in it."

What he referred to was no Mojave devil, but a devil called Syphilis that was second only to the Presbyterian devil in his mother's triology of punishers of evil-doers. Her third demon was Rum. The second devil was so horrible he could only be whispered about. He rotted the flesh of all those of Wanton Life, and his evil could be even transmitted to the innocent. So South Boy cleansed the knife that Come-into-the-Brush had given him with sand and water—white man's way, and with smoke—the Mojave way. Still he used his old knife, contaminated only by fish guts, to cut up the melons.

Suddenly he asked, "How long are we going to be gone?"

Havek shrugged his shoulders. "How can I tell?"

"You won't be back in time for school?"

Havek stripped the flesh off a fish and coughed. "Well, the agency police won't travel to the Piute country to find me. If I stay away a year or two years, I'll be a man grown when I come back. I'll have a new name. The white people at school will think Havek is dead—and this new Indian with a new name, he comes from elsewhere.

"I'm tired of school, anyway," he continued. "It's all right when you're small. Lots of boys to play with. But now I can talk English. I can read and write and figure money. No trader can cheat me. Why should I let them shut me up in a school for half of every day and make me work the other half on the farm?"

"Half a day!" cried South Boy. "Do you know what they're going to do to me? Put me in a school where they shut you up *all* day, until suppertime. And after supper they shut you up in your bedroom and make you study until they turn off the lights!"

Havek shook his head. "That would kill you. Quick."

"I know. The white boy at the Fort—you know—the superintendent's son. He told me all about that school. He said if they ever tried to send him back there he was going to run away to Mexico and live with the Cocopah."

Havek nodded. "Even the mud-eating Cocopah lead a better life than that." Then he added, "If we're gone long enough people will think you're dead, too."

It was then, as he sat biting the orange-colored flesh of the little melon down to the white rind that South Boy knew he had run away. He would pass forever out of the world of the white men and thereby rid himself of all its problems. It was a pretty bitter moment. He thought of the tree rolling down the river. He thought of the tears on his mother's face when she left him at the railroad station in Needles. He thought of the time she had cried for a day and a night in her darkened room when word came that her father had died.

Still, it would be a kinder thing to let her think he was dead, for he knew how bitter she was at the thought of his living in any other world than her own. Once last summer she had seen him talking to an Indian girl out on the road. When he got back to the house he heard her berating his father. "You get him out of here! You send him to school—I don't care whether you can afford it or not! I'd follow him to his grave rather than . . ."

And another time the Foreman came home roaring-drunk, a bullet in his leg, another man's blood on his shirt, and a dirty song on his lips—one of the few times South Boy had seen him completely happy. His mother was furious. "There's your son ten years from now if you don't get him out of this godless country. I'd rather see him dead . . ."

Well, he would be dead. He got up from the fire and went to roll his fishline so that Havek wouldn't see his tears. There he sat on the bank, slowly rolling up the cord, not thinking any longer, but just feeling a dumb, dull misery. How long, he didn't know. He was jerked out of the depth of his mood by a sharp whistle.

"Quick! Bring my bow and arrows!"

CHAPTER V

THE WOMEN

HAVEK stood on the bank two hundred yards away, staring at a group of dead, half-rotted stalks of a milletlike plant about ten feet out in the water. One of the stalks was wiggling spasmodically. South Boy, out of breath, handed him the bow and arrows.

Havek laid his poorest hunting arrow across his bow and waited. South Boy immediately pulled the box of crackers out of his shirt and got ready to jump. No word had passed between them, for each knew exactly what to do. A big fish was slowly working its way up that stalk, eating the green algae that clung to it. About ninety seconds later a lump the size of a big man's fist broke through the gray, semi-opaque water.

At the twang of the bowstring, South Boy leaped and lit spread-eagle with a tremendous splash. The fish started to roll over to shake free of the arrow but South Boy was right on top of it, his arm around it. The gyrating tip of the arrow almost knocked out his left eye. He gave a terrific heave, and the fish flew out and landed on the bank.

South Boy stood up, waist-deep, washing away slimy fish scales and mud from his hands, face, and shirt. His troubles had suddenly faded, and he felt good again. But he began to feel some concern about the cartridges in his gun, even though he had greased them well. He scrambled out of the water and looked the fish over. It was a native humpback sucker, soft of flesh and full of bones, weighing seven or eight pounds. Havek was stringing it on a slender willow pole. South Boy picked up Havek's bow and the arrow that had transfixed the sucker, put the box of crackers back in his shirt and started along the bank

He knew the chances were against getting another fish before they reached the Whisperer's camp, but he was not going to take the chance of soaking those cartridges again.

However he had not gone another two hundred yards before he saw a commotion among some water-killed weeds near shore and he loosened an exploratory arrow into the midst of it. The effect was terrific—something like an underwater explosion. Havek landed right in the midst of it, and came up in no more than two feet of water with a huge white fish in his arms.

"Salmon!" he gasped, clambering up the bank. "I saved my arrow, too."

The fish was no salmon, although it was popularly so called all along the river. It was a great chub, first cousin to the minnows found in all eastern streams, and an own brother to the Sacramento squawfish. A Yuma Indian once trapped one that weighed eighty pounds. This one weighed about twenty. A soft, poor, bony fish, but regarded as good food by the Mojaves because it had been in the river since the First Times.

Promptly strung on the pole and the pole resting on the boys' shoulders, the fish went swinging towards the Whisperer's.

The Whisperer's field lay in a horseshoe bend in the Snake lagoon a half-mile farther north—six or eight hoe-cultivated acres—a crazy quilt of odd patches of corn, beans, squash, pumpkins, a little wheat, and several kinds of melons, all growing furiously under the burning sun, their roots deep in seepage-soaked silt. Nowhere in the world was a field more productive.

In its midst the Whisperer was vigorously chopping weeds with a modern steel hoe; the sun glistened on the sweat that poured from his naked body, a bundle of long hair-ropes swinging pendulumlike across his back with each stroke of the hoe. In primitive times he would have used a wooden weed-cutter—otherwise his agricultural methods were those given to the Mojave by Mastamho.

When he caught sight of the boys, he dropped his hoe, clapped his hands together, grabbed his undershirt and pants from the ground and started on a shambling run for his rancheria which was built across the narrow neck of the horseshoe.

There was a winter house, which looked like a sand hill with a tunnel mouth, a "modern" house with a chimney, like a Mexican adobe, a large well built ramada, and three granaries that looked like great birds' nests atop log scaffoldings.

Seeing the Whisperer run, Havek looked puzzled. "Why didn't he wait for us?"

South Boy laughed. "On account of Maria. She'd give him hell if he stayed and talked to strangers with his pants off."

When they came within a few yards of the willow-roof an untidy fat woman with a widow's half-long hair came running to meet them, jabbering like an excited magpie about the fine large fish. The boys paid no heed to her. She was not the Whisperer's wife, but one of the inevitable poor relations that live in every prosperous camp. She paid little attention to the boys, either, but ran alongside the fish, patting and stroking them.

The Whisperer was sitting down, pulling on his undershirt, when they came under the shade, a big man, but not fat. On the far side of the shed sat Maria, cross-legged, a bowl full of little glass beads in her lap, and a bead loom across her knees. Eight or ten feet in front of her was a fat lump of a girl who was a younger duplicate of the widow. Maria said "Hello" with gloomy severity. The fat girl stared at the boys with slack-jawed stupidity. The Whisperer grinned a frank, delighted welcome while he buttoned his hastily donned pants. The widow petted the fish and yammered.

Havek and South Boy swung the pole off their shoulders and dropped the fish in front of the Whisperer.

The Whisperer squeaked, "Con-yaipa?" joyfully.

"Yes, for you," said South Boy. Whereupon the widow seized the fish and bore them away, yipping like a coyote, yelling for the girl to put the biggest pot in the fire hole. In spite of their fat and appearance of sloppy indolence, both women moved with the swift, surprising energy of Mojaves who have a definite job to do. The girl grabbed a pottery jar of five- or six-gallon capacity, ran to the lagoon, ran back with it dripping, set it in the fire hole, and pushed hot coals and ashes around it with a stick.

The widow ripped the fish off the pole, dashed water on them from the olla that hung suspended in the middle of the shed, rubbed them down with her hands, ran with them to the woodpile by the fire, chopped them into convenient chunks, and chucked the pieces, heads, tails, guts and all, into the pot. Still jabbering, she ran to fetch a sack half full of metate-ground corn meal, took a double handful and threw it in with the fish.

South Boy seated himself about five feet from the silent Maria and pulled the box of soda crackers out of his shirt and handed them over to her. He was a little ashamed of his gift, for what with sweat, water, and the general wear and tear of travel, the outside wrapper was almost obliterated and the box was badly battered. But the inner wrapper of oiled paper, put there by a farseeing manufacturer, had saved the contents.

Maria said, "Thank you," and looked pleased, but she did not smile like a real Mojave. She gravely opened the box, took two unbroken crackers from one end and passed the box back to South Boy, who, for reasons of his own, took his crackers from the opposite end and untouched by Maria's fingers. Then he tossed the box over to the Whisperer who selected two at random. Havek came next. He managed to find two unbroken. Then the box was seized by the widow and her fat daughter, who squalled like cats over the residue. All the others ate slowly and in dignified silence.

"They've got no more manners than pigs," said Maria in English like a white woman's. "The girl's never been to school.

Always lived way out in the brush and don't know anything. They're *his* relatives, not mine. But I'm going to see she goes to school if I have to break her neck."

All the time she talked she was swiftly stringing the small beads on her needle, or weaving them across the warp-threads of her loom.

"Say, I heard your mother died in California. Is that true?" The bald statement was shockingly un-Mojave.

South Boy's reaction was the same as though the words had been spoken by a white woman. "No," he snorted. "That's a story going around. She got well. She'll be back with cool weather."

"That's fine," said Maria. "Nice to have her back."

South Boy stirred uneasily. From the back of his mind came uncomfortable thoughts. Then for some reason he remembered the gun in his shirt and glanced down quickly to see if the bulge showed. If Maria saw it she would go down to the ranch the moment word came his mother had returned. She would report indignantly, "That boy of yours is wearing a belly-gun like a no-good Needles tinhorn." He didn't want to cause his mother additional pain.

It wasn't that Maria enjoyed malicious gossip, but she had a very strong sense of what white women considered wrong or wicked. Having been very wrong and wicked herself, she was ever eager in these later days to uphold white women's standards. She was an unending puzzle to South Boy and the Mojaves.

Maria was half-white. Her father had been one of the dragoons that had come to establish the Fort in 1859. For some unaccountable reason he had been legally married to her mother. The wedding must have been the dragoon's idea, for no Mojave woman in those still primitive times had ever heard of any kind of marriage ceremony. Mastamho had never taken the trouble to inaugurate weddings. If a man and woman liked each other they went off into the brush for a while, and if they decided they wanted to stay together, one of them moved in with the other's family until they could establish a camp of their own.

Maria was very proud of her legitimate birth, but the moral example of her parents had had little effect in her youth. After her father died—he had lived with her mother to the end— the railroad came to Needles, and Maria established herself in an adobe shack near the construction camp and made herself a mint of money (according to the Foreman) before fading beauty and the arrival of white competition forced her into retirement. Then she went to live with the Whisperer—a good-looking, industrious upstanding young Mojave whose only defect was the knife wound in his throat that had robbed him of his voice.

Among the Mojaves, Maria had much the same standing as a retired actress of great fame would have in a small town if she married a local boy and settled down to an exemplary life: a rich, industrious, strong-minded woman with an exotic past. Her manners were foreign, and to some extent her dress. She wore her hair parted in the middle and combed down on either side of her head, without the universal bangs of Mojave women. Her dresses were better-fitting, less full, and more nearly in the current American style, than those the Mojave women had been wearing since they had abandoned bark skirts for calico a generation or so earlier. All Mojaves regarded Maria with awe and respect, but nobody confided in her, because telling Maria anything was just like telling it to a white person.

South Boy's attitude towards Maria, and that of every other white male—except the preacher and one or two like him—was very much the same as the Mojaves'. But the white women . . .

To them she was Poisoned Flesh—in the words of South Boy's mother; but, because of her uncompromising rectitude during these recent years, she was a Soul Half Saved. They made it a point to speak to her kindly, from a distance, and urge her to seek Jesus. South Boy's mother even offered to take her down to the preacher in Needles in her own surrey, in spite of the fact that she was in perfect panic at the idea of coming so closely in contact with one undoubtedly possessed of the Syphilitic Devil—which might fly from the back seat where Maria would sit to the front seat and there attack either herself or South Boy.

Still, Maria was a brand worth snatching from the burning —with asbestos gloves. Maria always agreed with everything the Good Women said—up to the actual step of becoming a confessed Christian. She said it was too late. She had been too sinful. South Boy had a feeling that Maria knew that she would never get the amount of public attention as a Saved Soul that she was getting as a Brand to be Snatched.

Now all Maria had to do was to appear where two or three ladies were gathered together and within five minutes they would be standing around at a safe distance, weeping, begging her to come into the Fold. Maria managed to arrange most of these occasions when there would be three or four Mojaves in the middle distance telling one another that this Maria must certainly be a Person of Importance to have white women crying over her every time they met her—and even though it had been four or five years since her last relative had died.

As he sat there watching her swift, dexterous hands, South Boy pondered another possible reason why Maria wouldn't take the Preacher's hand. In spite of her foreign ideas, she was probably still too much of a Mojave to hold much store in rewards in Heaven or punishments in Hell. The Mojave's Heaven was no better than a pale, still land of shadows, and Hell was no worse than a rat's hole.

To be a Mojave—to have one God dead and one God on a permanent vacation—to have a Heaven without substance and a Hell without horror: there came an emptiness in the pit of South Boy's stomach as he thought about it.

Then he was distracted by a grimace of pain that swiftly crossed Maria's face. Punishment in this life for transgressions was entirely in accord with Mojave ideas, and it was stoically accepted. Maria had transgressed, by the Mojave code, by having intercourse with outlanders. Many had transgressed thus and were paying for it by barrenness and by having an invisible coyote gnawing at their bellies.

South Boy wondered if that was what Maria thought about it. He would have asked her outright if she had been a real Mojave; but Maria, like a white woman, would have been indignant.

She looked up at him sharply. "What's Havek talking to my man about?"

"A bow," said South Boy. "I need a good bow."

Maria nodded vigorously. "Yes, you're a lot better off hunting with a bow than with that big blunderbuss I see you packing sometimes. It's a wonder you haven't shot your head off."

Thus he completed his mission, which was to win Maria's approval of the bow-making.

The Whisperer had already pulled three or four long, seasoned staves of black willow out of the roof thatch, and he and Havek had selected one. South Boy had his own ideas and wanted to be in on the choosing. When he turned to go Maria said, "We have somebody else here—she's a surprise for you," but he thought very little about it and hurried over to the men.

Havek and the Whisperer sat side by side on the clean-swept, hard-packed adobe floor with the bow stave across their knees. It had already been partly worked. Both men examined it closely to determine the course of the grain. South Boy sat down on the other side of the Whisperer and laid his hand on the stave. It was given to him without a word. He nodded and passed it back. In his eight or nine years of experience in bow-making he had never seen a better one.

The Whisperer put his hand into a small pot in front of him full of broken glass and sharp chips of stone. He fingered around gingerly and brought out a fragment. He began scraping off long thin shavings with it, working with great speed and energy, singing to himself in his hoarse, croaking, whispering voice. He had been a great Dream-singer.

Havek and then South Boy selected sharp bits of glass and sat poised and ready, watching the Whisperer's flying scraper. Out of breath, the Whisperer rasped, "Take it," and shoved the bow to South Boy, tapping a long forefinger at the spot to be scraped. His eyes were dancing. South Boy scraped manfully. The sweat ran into his eyes and poured off his body. He scraped double-time to the Whisperer's muted song. South Boy felt good.

Maria was absorbed in her beadwork. The fat woman was talking endlessly to herself or anybody who might be listening, complaining of the heat, saying aloud everything that was passing through her stupid head. Every now and then she got up and dribbled a small handful of corn meal into the pot where the fish was cooking. The fat girl spent most of her time half hidden behind her mother, looking at Havek. Her stare was both vapid and impudent. Occasionally she got up and slouched over to the fire, where she took a sip of warm water from a small pot that stood by itself at the edge of the ashes. Her hair was as slovenly as her person. Out of the corner of his eyes, South Boy saw that the tattoo marks on her face were fresh. That fact, and the hot-water drinking, marked her as "a woman in her first forty days"; but he paid no attention to her. She came quite close to Havek and stared at him with looselipped concentration. Havek picked up a little stick and threw it at her.

The bow rapidly took shape under six swift hands. Sometimes three scrapers were working at one time. Sometimes the Whisperer took it in his own hands, feeling it over carefully. Twice he called for water and all three drank.

At last the bow was notched and strung with a thick sinew string. It was six feet long, almost six inches taller than South Boy. Then it was unstrung, and the Whisperer took it to scrape again—"to take out the bad bend." South Boy had thought that the draw was already perfect.

While this last and most delicate operation was taking place, the Whisperer said, "Look, a friend comes!" and pointed with his chin.

South Boy turned to look and saw coming out of the "modern" house a fine woman in her best clothes.

She wore a dress of purple silk that swept the ground as she walked. Around her shoulders was a close-fitting cape of beadwork, blue and white in color. Tied across her chest and flowing down her back was a *tahoma*—four large, yellow, figured silk handkerchiefs sewed together to make one large square. Her fine oval face was neither young nor old. Her complexion was a soft yellow-brown like the inside of the bark of the willow, showing she took care of herself, washed regularly, and kept out of the full sun. She walked through the shade like a ship sailing through smooth water, went first to the fire hole, examined the fish mush, added a handful of corn meal, then took four or five tortillas from a covered basket, put them into a pottery bowl, ladled a generous helping of red beans and salt meat from one of the several small pots on the fire, and came straight to South Boy with it, smiling, walking like a grand lady—very different she was indeed from either the wasted, exotic Maria, or the lumpy, sloppy, poor relations.

Everyone was watching South Boy now and grinning—even Maria. The lady smiled affectionately at South Boy as she handed him the food. She had pleasant little wrinkles around her eyes and mouth. Then she sat down directly in front of him, her hands in her lap, the yellow soles of her bare feet just showing on either side of her purple skirt.

"Her name is Heepa," called out Maria. "She is *my* relative."

South Boy said, "Thank you," to the lady in English, because he was too surprised to say anything else. He had no idea why he should be so honored until she called him "son," and then "little son." Then he knew she was a clan sister or possibly a blood sister to another Heepa, now dead, who had nursed him when he was a baby. He began to remember. This woman had married a southern Mojave and had gone to live down below Parker when he was still very small.

The lady, then, stood in the relation of a deputy foster mother. So she dressed up for him and fed him with her own hands. He was deeply proud to find himself related to a person of her quality. He folded meat and beans into a tortilla and ate hugely to show his appreciation. The lady was telling him how little, puny, and white he had been when he was a baby. She and her sister had cried over him because they thought he wouldn't live long. Now he was so tall . . .

The beans and meat were salty. They tasted good. He had sweat a great deal. He ate and listened to her soft voice. Havek and the Whisperer were being fed by the garrulous fat woman. South Boy was thinking how awful to find yourself related to her. Still, the Whisperer didn't seem to mind. He took what Fate dealt him in the line of relatives and thought little about it.

South Boy's eyes started to roll back in his head. He promptly lay down, there where he was, his head close to the purple silk skirt. He heard the lady say, "Almost a man, now," and for an instant her fingers touched his face. He was thinking he would like to tell her he was a Hawk-dreamer bound for high adventure, going to go into the wild north to harry the Piutes. That would give her great pride . . .

He went to sleep feeling very good. But he saw, when his eyes opened for the last time, that the objectionable fat girl had quit staring at Havek.

She was staring at him.

South Boy woke up four hours later. The sun was halfway down towards the Nevada mountains. It was still very hot, but the wind came in the usual fitful gusts of the afternoon and made it feel cooler. His first thought was to remember his dream; but it had been a worthless sort of white man's dream about being in California at the seashore with the ocean wind in his face, eating ice cream.

The lady in the purple dress sat with her back against a post, her eyes closed, her face composed. The fat woman and her daughter sprawled out—formless, dingy bumps in dirty calico. Maria in her clean faded gingham was propped against a farther post, head bent over her loom, her long hair hiding her shrewd, haggard face. Havek and the Whisperer slept belly down, and the bow—new, white, strung and ready—lay between them.

South Boy got up quietly, went to the olla suspended from the middle rafters and took a long drink. It was good. Everything was still. The gusts of wind driving little puffs of sand over and through the low, scattered brush between the camp and the mesa made only small noises. The talk of the distant river was far away. South Boy looked at the sky. It had a coppery tinge. There was a big storm in the far north and the wind had sent red silt into the high air. South Boy picked up his bow and tried its strong, even pull. Then he kicked Havek.

"Get up," he whispered in English. "Let's go. I don't want to have to eat any of that fish mush."

A moment later the Whisperer rolled over and saw South Boy leaning on his bow, impatient to travel. He jumped up and pulled eight arrows out of the thatch and laid them on the hard ground at the boy's feet.

"Take four," he whispered. "They are hawk-feathered." And he grinned.

So he knew. South Boy glanced over at Maria and saw that she still slept; but the lady in purple, his deputy mother, had her eyes open. She smiled at him in great pride. She knew then —at least something. South Boy leaned over and selected four of the straightest and best arrows. He would find iron somewhere, and make points. Then his war arrows would be better than Havek's.

Havek got up, took a long drink, and was ready to go.

"Wait, I must give you something," said the lady, very softly. The three men waited by the edge of the shade. The Whisperer said, "Good dreaming!" which meant good luck. His black eyes were shining. The lady came hurrying back with a clean salt sack. She had put a quart of parched corn and hulled squash seeds into the bottom of the sack and then filled it with screw beans that had lain for a year in a hole in the ground, so that they were very sweet. She said, "Travel lightly, son," when she gave him the sack. South Boy did not know the way to thank her, so he shook her hand white-fashion and mumbled quickly, "Thank you—goodbye."

The two boys started off at a slow trot through the short brush that edged the cultivated land and so to the return bend of the lagoon where big mesquite trees grew along its bank.

South Boy had seen the fat girl go hustling across the field towards the mesquite while he was selecting the arrows, but he had thought nothing about it at all. So he was entirely surprised when she stepped out from behind the third or fourth tree directly in front of him and seized him by his shirt, almost jerking him off his feet. She didn't look at him. Her tousled hair hung down with the mock modesty a woman from the brush affects on such occasions. South Boy yipped like a frightened dog, jerking away from her, almost tearing his shirt.

"Dirt face," he shrieked, fanning the air between them with his new bow. "Fat belly!" He was panic-stricken. The Presbyterian devil and the devil called Syphilis were snatching at him.

To make matters worse, Havek was doubled up with laughter, crying out: "You fat fool! Didn't you know this little boy isn't grown yet?" South Boy swished his bow and shrieked more insults at both of them. Everybody from the camp came running to see what the row was about.

The Whisperer got there first, squealing and bending over in cracked-voice mirth. Behind him came the fat woman. When she saw her mother, the girl threw back her head, pointed her finger at South Boy and howled like a wolf. South Boy had not only spurned her foully but said insulting things. The fat woman chattered like an angry monkey and started throwing clods at him.

Back of her was the lady in purple. She was laughing moderately. The girl wanted the boy, but the boy didn't want any such ugly lump of a girl. It was amusing, but her restrained manner was a reproof to these people who were creating an unseemly fuss about it.

Back of her came Maria. Maria, ex-denizen of a Needles brothel, showed herself wholly for conventional "white" morality. She told the girl off in sharp bitter words for immodesty and indecency, and said to South Boy in English: "You tell your mother this never happened in my camp. Tell her I'm going to teach this girl how to act decent if I have to skin her." She then spoke bitter words in Mojave. Whereupon the girl's mother stopped throwing clods at the boy and started throwing them at Maria.

The last South Boy heard as he ran away was the girl howling, and the fat woman and Maria obscenely screaming names of each other's dead relatives.

South Boy ran in a blind panic for fifteen minutes until he was heat-dizzy and gasping for breath. Then he caught a blurred glimpse of the lagoon through a break in the mesquite and stumbled towards it, more with the idea of washing away the polluting touch of the fat girl than giving himself relief from the heat. He dropped his equipment and hit the water with a terrific splash, found himself on the soft bottom and stayed there for a full minute, rubbing his hands futilely over the front of his shirt. Then he came up to the surface through no particular volition of his own and automatically struck out for the water's edge. There he sat, splashing water on himself, washing away the bottom mud and the unseen pollution with it until the racing of his heart ceased and his breath came back.

The warm air blew cool on his wet clothes and he began to

reason away his fears. He had no true facts on which to base his reason, but he remembered a conversation he had had with the Foreman about the possibilities of sterilizing the back seat of the surrey, if and when Maria rode in it on the Soul-saving journey, and thereby protecting future occupants from a possible attack of the devil-whose-name-is-whispered.

The Foreman just laughed and laughed. When he got his breath back he said, "Son, you do pick up the damnedest notions." After that he gave a long and complete discourse in plain language about venereal infections and concluded with the statement: "Take it from a man that knows, there is only one way to pick up anything like that, and it ain't from sitting down in a carriage seat."

So South Boy sat in the mud slowly thinking over what the Foreman had told him. The panic eased out of his mind. It didn't stand to reason he was in any danger because the girl had grabbed his shirt. The Foreman had said: "Keep your nose clean, but don't take no stock in them wild ideas of your mother. She's a lady. Naturally, she's ignorant."

South Boy climbed up the bank, terrifically angry with himself for losing his dignity. He should have just laughed at the girl. He made the best of a bad situation by ignoring Havek. He cut a piece of fishline and tied both ends to his provision sack, slipping the loop over his shoulder. He picked up his bow and arrows. They gave him a thrill of pride, in spite of his shame. He started slowly off through the short brush, his eyes on the ground, his face burning.

He had not gone a hundred yards before Havek came running up, kicking a small, round desert gourd ahead of him. Havek loosened an arrow at it and sent it bounding away with a glancing blow. This was their old game. South Boy couldn't resist it. He loosened an arrow and split the gourd, and pride lifted his heart.

Soon they were running side by side, kicking gourds and

shooting at them, yipping like young coyotes, the past far behind them. They cried aloud at the excellence of their bows
and bragged up each other's marksmanship, declaring no two
grown men in the valley could shoot so well.

Chapter VI

THE LAST WAR CLUB

THE VISIT to Yellow Road's camp was an unexpected interlude as far as South Boy was concerned. As he ran along in the hot wind making pride for himself with his arrows to crowd out the indignity he had suffered in the matter of the fat girl, he didn't notice that they were heading northeast instead of northwest until he looked up and saw the dun cliff of the mesa right ahead. Up on the rim was a camp, a very poor one. Only a ramada of six posts with a brushy, poorly made roof of mixed brush, and a single bird's-nest granary.

So he asked, "What are we doing here?"

"I forgot to tell you," said Havek, who had already started up the switchback trail to the camp. "We stop for a little while to see my father's uncle. He's Yellow Road, called El Capitan. He'll be dead before we get back; so I want to see him once more. Besides, he's a very great captain. He might tell us something."

South Boy was surprised into silence. He had heard many stories about the almost legendary Yellow Road, but he had thought him already dead.

The two boys found the old Indian sitting with his back against the northeast corner post of the ramada, farthest from the sun, a tall, gaunt old man, the color of half-dry adobe dusted with ashes, naked except for a loincloth and a wild tangle of long gray hair. There were only two visible pieces of property under the shed. One was a small olla containing pounded mesquite beans steeping in water that stood at the old man's right hand; the other, a great war club, shaped like

a cooper's maul or a big bung starter, suspended by a rawhide
thong from a knot on the post behind him.

South Boy knew this wasn't ordinary poverty. Yellow Road
had been both a great hota and a great war chief; but now,
considering he had long since outlived his usefulness, he had
retired into voluntary poverty to wait for the oblivion of death,
as Mastamho had waited with folded arms for transformation
into a fish hawk. Such was customary with great men who
lived too long.

And the war club over his head—South Boy had never before seen one though every singing and every long tale was full
of them—that marked Yellow Road as belonging to a time
that was long gone. In a little while now, this last war club
would be burnt on the same pyre with its owner. Then all
clubs and all of the clubbers would belong wholly to legend.

As soon as Yellow Road began talking, South Boy realized
that he belonged to an older and in many ways much different
generation than those now considered "old men"—the hota of
last night's singing, for instance—who were the present keep-
ers of tradition.

He had said nothing until the boys sat down before him and
Havek had laid his bundles of arrows proudly in front of him.
The old man took one look at the iron points and said, "So
you have learned this shameful, newfangled business of lying
in the brush and shooting people who can't see you! So your
arm is so weak and your bow is so poor you must have points
on your arrows!"

Havek said: "We go name-traveling through Piute country,
and the Piutes are at war. They've got Winchester rifles."

Yellow Road shook his head, gasped for breath, and to relieve himself took a drink of mesquite-bean gruel from the pot.

"Nobody knows how to do anything properly now—nobody. Traveling is one thing. War is another. This shoot-in-
the-back business that people learned from the Apaches a while
ago and call small-men war—that's another thing again. Wait,

I'll tell you—" He took another drink from the olla and waited to get his breath.

"Let me tell you the proper way of traveling. It was given me. I know it.

"If a man wants to win himself honor by traveling to friendly people, like the Yuma, to the south, or the Yavapai, to the east, or the Zuñi, to the northeast, or the Vanyume, over west in the Tehachapi Mountains—then he strips himself naked and fasts half the day and runs day and night, not sparing himself at all. If he carries goods for trading, that is a different matter—I'm speaking of traveling for honor and name-winning. He runs as fast as he can, calculating his strength, so he will just last until he gets to the friendly village. Then he falls. The life is almost out of him. If he dies, he has done a Great Thing. But, being a real man, he usually lives when the women come and pour water over him. Then he takes a little water in his mouth. Then a little gruel. Then he sleeps one or two days, and then his friends feast him and he tells them his new name.

"Now if he travels to the country of a suspicious unfriendly people like the Indians on the California coast, or the Hopi, or the Havasupai to the north, he runs fast, but he sleeps and eats a little to save himself. When he comes to the town of such people, he runs fast so he will appear covered with sweat and the people will think he has run all the way. He carries no weapon, but in this case he has a staff in his hand. He goes boldly to the best house in the town and leans on his staff, shouting: 'Huh! Wah! Bring water and we'll be friends. Shoot arrows at me, and the clubbers will come!'

" 'This is a Mojave,' the people will say, 'because only they dare do this.' Usually they give him water and later food, and something to show he has been there—a bow, or a few beads, or something.

"If they are foolish and attack him, he jumps inside the house and kills everybody he can with his staff, breaking heads, legs, or arms until they shoot him down or cut him down. He dies singing the songs that he dreamed, knowing the clubbers will come and avenge him, killing everybody they catch and burning the town.

"Now if he travels to an enemy town—still he runs naked with only a stick in his hand, or maybe nothing. But he does not exhaust himself. He goes cautiously. He goes at night. At night he enters the town as I in my youth entered the Hopi town of Oraibi when those people were angry with us over a matter of trade.

"I climbed the high hill at Oraibi. Houses are piled on top of houses there. I went everywhere cleverly, like the shadow of a ghost. I stole a sack of meal from a house full of people. I went over housetops and through streets, through houses, through estufas where medicine men slept, leaving a yellow trail of meal behind me. I could have killed ten, but I killed no one. I was not making war. I was name-traveling. So I stole a doll dressed after the Hopi style, just to show where I'd been. And I took the name of Yellow Road, as everybody knows."

The old man drank from the olla again. Both Havek and South Boy murmured in Mojave. "A Great Thing! Surely, a Great Thing!"

"But the Piutes have guns!" said Havek.

"Guns!" croaked Yellow Road. "I'll tell you something. The Spaniards had guns! When I was small, my father and a dozen more went to Santa Barbara by the ocean to trade with the Spaniards. They had guns, and a fort, and soldiers. The Mojaves didn't have even their clubs. They had only a few bows and some hunting arrows, for they had come to trade. But a Spaniard tried to cheat a Mojave and then insulted him, so the Mojave slapped his face and because the Spaniard was puny, his neck broke.

"The Spaniards fired on the naked Mojaves, wounding two. The Mojaves yelled, 'Clubs! Clubs!' And as they had no clubs they took sticks of oak firewood and chased the Spaniards into their fort. The Mojaves kept them shut up in there for about a week, and then Mission Indians were sent out with presents to pay for the wounded. So the Mojaves took a few horses to carry the presents and went home, laughing."

"The Piutes have Winchester rifles, and six-shooters, too," Havek pointed out.

The old man made no answer, but closed his eyes; and his laborious breathing became painful to watch, until the wind came and cooled him and stirred his long hair.

When he opened his eyes he skipped over the reference to modern firearms. "I have told you of proper traveling. Now I'll tell you of proper war. One of you hand me down my club."

Both boys sprang up, but South Boy, being lighter and swifter, laid his hand on it first. The club had been carved out of the black heart of a mesquite log so that it was all of a piece, handle and all. To South Boy it had a smooth, greasy feel that came from much rubbing and handling by sweaty hands.

The old man took it and held it up before his face. "With this the Mojaves made their name feared from the Pueblos east of the Zuñi to the Western Ocean, and from the big Salt Lake in the north to the river of the Yaquis in the south. Everywhere a Mojave could travel naked and alone for honor and experience, or just for trade, because everyone knew that in the Mojave country there were clubs just like this one. We never sent war parties out to loot and run, like Apaches and coyotes. We had everything we wanted at home. When we sent out a party, it was to avenge a brother and thereby keep our honor great. And everyone knew when the Mojaves fought the fight would end in one of three ways: All the enemy would be killed, the enemy would run away, or all the Mojaves would be killed. A war chief never had to account for his lost men when he came home. He reported to his people, 'The enemy is gone, their town is burnt.' "

By this time Yellow Road had lapsed into the swift, jerky phrases of a formal oration. "In the last *good* war I was the leader. The Cocopah killed a Yuma traveler. Our cousins (the Yuma) said, 'Send us a hundred men.' I took a hundred *real* men. Big men with clubs like this. I took twenty-five small men with straight bats to break heads. I took fifty Chemehuevi, too, mounted on horses. They were our scouts. Mojaves ran on foot all the long journey. Being big men, horses can't carry them swiftly in hot weather.

"So we joined the Yuma at Algadones in Mexico and we ran two days to find the Cocopah. Our scouts found them. They had a trench and an embankment all around their town. They had guns.

"We had bows and plain arrows, but we didn't use them. In the last hour of darkness, we charged their fort in a single line of clubs with the small men and the scouts behind us. They fired one volley, killing some of us, and then we were among them.

"Now here is the proper way to use a club. You charge. You seize your enemy by the hair. You thrust the club up, thus! Smash his face! Then you throw your man over your shoulder for the small men to finish with their straight clubs, or cut off his head with their knives.

"In five minutes the Cocopah all ran. Among their dead was a short-haired Mexican army captain who had come to show them how to fortify their town against us. Then we called out to the Cocopah, 'You are our cousins by blood. We won't kill any more of you, but you must never harm travelers!' We took all the horses we could find to carry our wounded, and we took six girls for slaves, and we went north to Algadones, carrying the heads of several of the slain. And there we rested and ate big meat, and smoked ourselves clean all over and bathed so we would not take the curse of blood and death back to our own country.

"There the man-who-was-chosen skinned the heads of the enemy—completely, face, and all, and tied them to a long pole that he carried. He was unclean and they were unclean. No one went near them. He watched the two slave girls, too. The other four we gave to the Yuma, for it was their traveler who had been killed. The slaves were unclean. Nobody touched them, except to keep them from running away."

So far Yellow Road had been telling what actually happened, but at this point, after he had drunk from the olla and wiped his mouth with the back of his hand, he began singing from the cycle of Dream-singing called "Nichiva," which gives the account of the return of the First War Party. But South Boy knew that Mojave ritual was so bound down to the tradition of the First Times, that the actual procedure of Yellow Road's party wouldn't have varied greatly from that set down in the song.

Yellow Road sang of the cloud of dust flying overhead that heralded the party's return. How the people shouted when they saw it. How they sent four alyah (men who dressed and behaved like women) to meet the warriors and aid the unclean trophy-bearer on whose pole the long hair of the head-skins waved and danced in the summer wind. How a hota came forth and invited all the warriors to a dance and a feast, and how he likewise offered a small house and a patch of garden to the captive slaves.

These girls lived a strange life thereafter. Technically they were the slaves of the host who took charge of them; but he never made them work, nor did he go near them or have anything to do with them except to see that they didn't run away. They were treated much like animals in a zoo. Mojaves came from long distances to watch these foreign women, often tossing them bundles of food.

If they got tired of being on exhibition, they could ask the hota to take them to the river and immerse them. If they were good girls and had not tried to run away for a long time, he would do it. Then they would be considered Mojaves and could live with any man who wanted them. But even then, they usually died virgins because all the men were afraid of them.

In the "Nichiva" singing there were many verses about the status of slave girls. Then it described the pole with the head skins standing in the ground in the middle of the dancing place. How the men and women danced around it, their faces painted black and yellow, their hair stiff with white clay and alkali—dancing in many groups, each in a different manner according to which cycle of Dream-singing its leader sang. Some clapped hands, some shook rattles, some danced to drumbeats made on a basket or a water jar. All this was in the "Nichiva" singing in great detail.

When the old Indian stopped he was very tired, and it was hard for him to get his breath. When he did he said: "They ate good at the feast. I was there. Now I am weak because I have not eaten for a long time. I need big meat and there is none here."

It occurred to South Boy that the old man might actually be starving.

Still grumbling about "big meat," Yellow Road drank some of the water and chewed a little of the bean fiber with his few poor teeth and spat it out with a grimace. Then he began the story of the first defeat the Mojaves suffered in tribal history.

Again a Yuma traveler had been murdered and again the killers had been a kindred tribe, this time the Maricopa—over in the Salt River valley. With the Maricopa lived the remnant of the Colorado River tribes that the Mojave and the Yuma had ruined in war and driven east across the desert. Some of these had killed the lone Yuma.

The Yuma, always a small tribe, sent eighty-two clubbers on a punitive expedition, the Mojave sent two hundred, and they were joined by a hundred Yavapai and a hundred and fifty Apache, all mounted.

The Maricopa knew they were coming and called on their friends the Pima, who were club fighters like the Mojave, and a very numerous people. They sent the Maricopa four hundred men who fought in solid phalanx behind big bullhide shields. The Apache horsemen charged first and fought like lions for about five minutes, having several horses killed and many men wounded; but when they found the Pima-Maricopa line would not break they fled. The Yavapai charged with the Apache. Being half Mojave and half Apache, they fought for a longer time and lost ten men before they ran. The Mojave and the Yuma, being on foot, struck next. They broke the line of Pima shields again and again, killing a hundred men.

But the Pima always re-formed. No other alien people had ever done that before in the history of Mojave warfare.

"Then," said Yellow Road, "I called to the Yuma. I said, 'They are too many, and we are too far from our own country!' But the Yuma were all dead but two. They had thrust themselves into the midst of the Pima and killed until they died. Nobody else fought like that but our people and the Pima. The Mojave lost forty men killed, and there was not a man among them but carried some wound . . ."

The defeated Mojave retreated for eight days through Yavapai country and through the land of the Walapai. The Walapai stood on their hills and jeered at them, and the Mojaves, too wounded and weary to punish them, went home to sulk and brood. This was in the spring of 1858.

Out of this jeering a greater evil was to befall. In August of that year a large immigrant train, the first contingent of Iowans to migrate to southern California, came down Lieutenant Beale's new trail through north-central Arizona and when they were camped at the river crossing where Fort Mojave now stands, the Walapai came and again taunted the Mojave, and dared them to attack the whites. And the Mojaves, still brooding over their defeat, did attack, killing eighteen people and stealing over six hundred head of cattle, driving the emigrants back the way they had come—and no others ever came down that trail.

Thus the Mojaves gained back their prestige—for a little

while. Then the soldiers came—the first hostile invasion of the Mojave valley.

Yellow Road said nothing of how the rifle fire of the soldiers mowed down the ranks of the Mojave clubbers. He ended his story cursing the Walapai, naming their dead grandfathers. He closed his eyes. He said: "I am weak. My shadow is weak. I need meat."

By and by he said: "So you are going into the Piute country. You will stay by the trail and kill Apache-fashion and think you are big men. There has been too much Indians killing Indians. That is why we are weak.

"Small-men war," he groaned. "Iron-point arrows. Thus we come to imitate coyotes when the days of our greatness are ended."

There was a weary, wind-driven silence for some time as the old man sat death-still, the black war club lying across his legs, its handle resting against his skeleton-thin knees.

He said, "Big meat," twice, without opening his eyes.

South Boy stared at the old man. A young person could live on mesquite beans and even get fat, but an old man with few teeth might starve.

He looked around to see two women coming up the trail burdened down with carrying-nets full of long white mesquite-bean pods. They went to the bird's-nest granary, climbed the low scaffolding, and dumped the contents of their nets into it. They were fat enough, but they had teeth.

"Bring me my gun," said the old man suddenly.

One of the women pulled an old single-shot Springfield rifle out of the thatch and brought it to him, laying it across his thighs.

As ancient as the rifle was, it looked outlandishly modern in the lap of the last of the clubbers. Probably it was a relic of the eighties, when the government had armed the now friendly Mojaves against a possible spread of Apache and Yavapai raids to the west. Anyhow, Yellow Road had a rifle and was fumbling big, finger-length cartridges out of the folds of the rag bound around his waist. He found four. He looked at Havek. "My eyes won't see and my legs won't carry me, and there is no man here to shoot me that big meat."

South Boy watched Havek out of the corner of his eyes and saw him squirm. One of the best bow-shots in the valley, he had fired a rifle only once in his life and then he had been knocked flat and had missed the target by twenty feet. He looked at South Boy pleadingly, knowing very well that the white boy had been having expert instruction in the use of just such a rifle from the Mormonhater for some two years.

"I'll use my arrows," said Havek uncomfortably.

"Then I'll starve," said Yellow Road. "The wild horse stays in the open where he can watch from far off."

South Boy let Havek fret awhile, in memory of his recent laughter, and then said, "Give me the gun." The old man said nothing. So South Boy took it and picked up one after another of the cartridges, selecting one in which the powder rattled freely. He kept but one because he knew he would never get a second shot with that rifle.

With the rifle in his hand, South Boy raised his head and stuck out his chest and spoke in the manner of a war captain giving orders. "Somebody carry my sack and my bow. Somebody show me where the wild horse grazes." And he started off down the trail without looking back. He had good reason to hurry, because the sun was almost down.

Before he was halfway down to the flat he began to have an uncomfortable, ashamed feeling. He'd made a show-off play. He had blackened Havek's face because Havek had laughed at him in the matter of the fat girl. A big man, like Yellow Road, would have done the thing simply and in good taste. South Boy felt very small and discontented with himself as his feet struck the soft ground of the flat and the white man's worries were on him again, full cry.

The rifle was old and rusty. It probably wouldn't shoot

straight. The barrel might even be so foul that it would blow out its breech. So he stopped, flipped the breechblock up and looked down the barrel. His heart sunk into his belly. He could not see through the bore at all.

Well, there was no turning back, for he knew there would be no use trying to explain to an old Indian that a rifle was no good as long as it was possible to crowd a cartridge into the chamber and close the breech.

He heard one of the women chirping at him from the trail behind, and he looked back to see her pointing northwest. He went with leaden feet to the first clump of arrowweeds and broke off one. He thrust the butt end down the barrel and pulled the leafy end through.

Much to his surprise, the arrowweed came out full of black grease instead of rust; so he pulled two or three more through the barrel and looked down the muzzle.

The bore was so clean it looked new. Immediately Yellow Road became an even greater man in South Boy's eyes. He was not only a great Mojave, but he possessed the white man's virtue of taking care of his gun.

South Boy looked back over his shoulder and saw Havek and the two women about a hundred and fifty yards behind, traveling silently. One of the women chirped again and raised her arm, flexing her wrist and throwing her hand forward to show that the horse was straight ahead and not too far away.

He signed them all to keep well back and went slowly on with the wind blowing his face in hot, fitful gusts. That was good. The horse couldn't smell him. But the wind blew spindrifts of fine sand that cut down vision, and whenever the wind stopped the heat waves danced up from the gray-white ground and distorted everything. And the sweat kept running into his eyes.

Just ahead was a spread of gravel that had been brought down from the mesa by past cloudbursts pouring through a wash to his right. South Boy bent low and threaded his way cautiously among the boulders on the gravel spread. There he caught his first glimpse of the horse. He immediately got down on his belly and crawled from one small, hot boulder to the next, then to a smoketree. Then to a sotol-weed growing on the edge of the soft ground.

The horse was grazing around a lone mesquite at the very edge of a small barranca that passed through a salt-grass flat almost a quarter of a mile away. He was a fat young mustang, dark chestnut with a white patch on his rump and another on his nigh shoulder. He browsed around the tree like a wild horse, snatching a mouthful of beans or leaves, then throwing his head up to look around him and sniff for enemies. Being away from the herd, he was extra-shy. He favored his off forefoot very slightly.

South Boy slowly crawled out onto flat ground so hot it burnt his belly, inching along towards another sotol-weed a hundred yards ahead. His eyes stung and his head was swimming. Back of the weed, he shoved the hindsight up one notch with his thumb.

There was a bunch of alkali-killed sage fifty or sixty yards farther on. Blindly and rebelliously he crawled towards it. He thought he would die before he thrust the barrel of the rifle through the dead bush so that it rested on the hummock of earth out of which the bush had grown.

Through sweat and tears and dancing heat he saw the horse stretch his neck out for a bunch of beans growing high—a fine alert horse—a good horse for anybody. As he cocked the big, clumsy hammer, he was thinking what a fine thing it would be to have that horse in the corral back home. It would come nickering along the fence to meet him—glad to see him.

All at once he felt that there could be nothing worse in the world than to shoot that horse—any horse—a horse was a friend. Then he saw the face of the old man back under the ramada, thin, gray, starving. A great man. There could be nothing worse than to let that man starve.

Why was it he was being put between two evils like this? Twice in the same day. Either he should let them send him away to a world that he dreaded like death, or he must break his mother's heart—leave her lying face down on her bed, sobbing into her pillow. Either he must shoot this splendid animal, or he must let the old man starve.

The mustang jerked his head down. He was going to run. The foresight was on that white spot—the heat waves were dancing and wriggling between. The horse jumped. South Boy had already pulled the trigger.

He got up rubbing his shoulder, the world spinning around him. He couldn't see, but he heard the cry, "Kwee-ee-ee-Kwi-i-i-va!" from the women. Then they came, yelling, "Pee-leel-leel-leel," like women at a scalp dance. They ran past him waving big knives, and jumped into the barranca where the horse had fallen.

Havek came up and said, "Look, they gave us bullhide sandals." South Boy was too sick to talk, so he sat down and put on the pair of sandals Havek gave him. By and by he said, "Leave my sack and bow and take the rifle to the women." Painfully he got up, and slowly he walked away, keeping his eyes on his feet so that he wouldn't see the women gutting the horse.

He was a half-mile along with his misery before Havek caught up with him. They traveled a quarter of a mile farther, then Havek said in great admiration, "You didn't brag or anything."

South Boy dropped his equipment and hid his face in his hands. Havek walked on in deference to what he thought was modesty.

Some time later they came to a gourd patch, and Havek flicked a gourd ahead and shot an arrow at it. South Boy couldn't resist. He shot an arrow, too, and the load of trouble and shame gradually dropped from him as they traveled on, shooting arrows until the sun sank and it was too dark to see.

Chapter VII

PAINTED HORSES

They slept that night in the middle of a little playa at the far end of the Snake lagoon. Some time after midnight when the bright moon was in mid-sky, South Boy woke out of a sound sleep, sweating profusely and full of dread. He called out to Havek, and Havek promptly sat up, saying, "Huh? What did you dream?"

"Nothing," said South Boy. "But it came to me that here we are traveling to a strange country we know nothing about."

"Shut up and go to sleep," Havek told him. "I thought you had dreamed something important."

"No, but we ought to ask questions and make plans. This is a silly thing coming into a strange country like two blind men. What's the war up there about? Just where is it? Where in the north are we going, and just what are we going to do?"

"What difference! Our dreams are good. We can't go wrong. Shut up and go to sleep." Havek rolled over on his belly, spread himself out like a starfish, and went to sleep.

"There I go worrying like a white man again!" South Boy told himself. So he lay watching the great low stars awhile, then went to sleep.

He awoke again with the first light, feeling good. He went down to the lagoon to drink and wash and replaster his head.

Havek got up with a grunt a moment later, shucked off his clothes before his eyes were entirely open and jumped into the lagoon. South Boy untied the mouth of his sack and began ruminating on sweet, brown screw beans, spitting out the fiber and hard seeds with noisy gusto. Here he was on the brink of adventure. There was but one Mojave rancheria between them

82

and the wild, empty, northern country that stretched for hundreds of miles ahead of them. He began thinking about Name-traveling and small-men war, and how the two had got all mixed up. He remembered Yellow Road's talk, and he had a painful flood of memory pictures of the horse-killing.

"Name-traveling the old way was the best," he said aloud. "We could do a Great Thing in the Piute country without killing anybody."

But still there were Piutes, war-mad, ready to kill on sight. A bullet would be the best thing he could expect of them. If they caught him while he was still alive, they would put one arrow through his guts and spread-eagle him on a bed of cholla cactus by a red ants' nest. The women and the children would poke out his eyes with sticks. All the details he knew by heart from the Mojaves.

Why, then, wouldn't it be a good thing to shoot a few Piutes? Like killing sidewinders, only more dangerous, therefore more sporting.

So he was all confused in his mind when Havek came back, dressed, wet and grinning, his own head mud-packed and tied up in a handkerchief.

He took a handful of screw beans and said: "The Travelers' road starts here. The war trail starts here. It's a long way to the Piute country, but from now on we travel as though a bullet might come out of every bush."

In about twenty minutes on a fast trail they came to the outpost rancheria and approached it with great caution as though it were the first camp of the enemy. There were two men and two women working in the field of corn and melons—vigorous half-young people. The men were chopping weeds with hoes, the women were gathering beans in a patch on the far side.

"My cousin and my father's first wife's grandson," Havek whispered. "Fast runners and keen-eyed men, both of them. If I get chased, you stay hid. I'll lose them in the brush and double back."

"You'll get your butt skinned," warned South Boy, viewing the field with an eye of the expert. "The cornstalks and the big weeds grow too scattered in that field. No good cover."

Havek dropped his weapons and stepped out into the field. Cornstalks grew irregularly in bunches of two and three, widely scattered among the watermelon vines. There were small melons and a few big melons, each covered with a little stack of dead weeds to keep off the sun. There was hardly hiding place for a very clever jack rabbit, but Havek faded into that field before he had gone fifty yards.

South Boy was lost in admiration. Never had he seen anything so well done. He thought of the heroes in the Great Tales and the Dream-singing that were always disappearing and traveling underground. By golly, that's what they must have meant, South Boy thought, a good job of belly-sneaking like that! Havek might be traveling underground for all a keen eye could see.

Out in the middle of the field the two men chopped weeds in rhythmical accord, their long hair-ropes swinging across their backs. Five minutes later they both stopped, wiped their faces, looked back at the newly risen sun, leaned on their hoes and exchanged a few words. Then they bent to their tasks again and their hair began to swing.

Suddenly South Boy's heart jumped up into his throat and stuck there. He saw two cornstalks sway in momentary agitation. Right behind the men! "Well, the damn fool!" he whispered in infinite admiration.

Then nothing. Not a sound, not a movement in the still, hot morning light, except the swaying of the hoers and the slow, hunching progress of the women in the bean patch. A dove cooed far away in the mesquite, and from over beyond the Mojaves' ramada a rooster crowed.

Ten breath-taking minutes, and Havek materialized at almost the same spot where he had disappeared. He came bent far over, panting, his strained face sweat-drenched, and clutched to his middle was a long green watermelon of some thirty pounds.

He rolled the melon under the low boughs of the mesquite that hid South Boy and flopped down beside it to get his breath.

South Boy was open-mouthed, pop-eyed, dumfounded. He considered himself a well schooled hand at the ancient game of raid-the-enemy, but this exhibition of skill was something undreamed of.

"Did you see me wiggle the cornstalks?" Havek panted.

South Boy nodded in wordless applaud. He dug out his great clasp knife and split the melon. It was dead-ripe. The heart was crimson and still cool from the night. He slashed a chunk out of it and handed it to Havek—an offering.

Havek slowly sucked the sweet juice, thoughtfully watching the men in the field. "Those are my kin," he said. "I know them. You know them. Smart, wide-awake men. Why, if I can cross such a field as that and snatch a melon from right under the rumps of such men as those, there isn't a horse or a woman in the Piute country that's safe from me."

"You leave women alone. You'll burn here, and you'll burn hereafter. I know. I've been told," said South Boy.

"Yes—well, I know foreign women are bad. Make it a horse or a gun, then. They've got fat, filthy, ugly-looking women, anyhow."

They ate the great heart out of the melon, dozed like gorged snakes for a half-hour, eased their bellies, slept another hour, and sat in great content, watching the field. A little while later the men stopped, shouldered their hoes, called to the women, and headed for camp.

"Are you empty enough to run?" asked Havek.

South Boy immediately slipped the string of his grub sack over his shoulder, picked up his bow and arrows, and ducked out from under the branches.

Havek's intention was only to create a minor confusion and perhaps an interesting chase, wherein they would get valuable practice in the art of losing a pursuing enemy. He raised the long yell of the Chemehuevi from behind the mesquite and threw a broken half of the melon into the field. He gave the Chemehuevi yell because he thought the men would be more certain to give chase if they thought they had been tricked by semistrangers from across the river.

But the result was entirely unexpected. The men didn't drop their hoes and come running, shouting curses, leaping over the low corn. They ran to their camp, directly and silently, bent low, keeping their hoes in their hands. The women, already at the ramada, broke into shrill screams and began pulling weapons out of the thatch. The men kept their hoes in their hands until the women ran to them, giving one a rifle and the other a shotgun. Three of them immediately ran over to the hillock of sand covering the winter house—the highest place around there. One woman ran back to the ramada, her tahoma flying straight behind her. From the thatch she snatched bows and a bundle of arrows and joined the others. The other woman came down from the housetop and returned with an axe.

One of the men began booming in a great bass voice.

"Chemehuevi! Awahy! Awh-wa-a-aay!"

That "awahy" meant "foreign." Foreign Chemehuevi is the Mojave name for all up-river and plateau Piutes.

The Mojaves hadn't mistaken Havek for a "tame" Chemehuevi. They thought the yell came from an up-river hostile of the same blood and language. Being frontiersmen, they put themselves immediately in the best possible position for defense, and sent a warning booming down the valley.

South Boy and Havek faded into the brush, running like cats, picking out each footfall, thanking their dreams that the hard ground left no trail. They heard an answering from far down the valley.

"You're a damn fool!" said South Boy when they'd put a mile of open mesquite flat between them and the rancheria. "There will be scouts out in a hour, and the agency police, too, on horse and on foot. By golly, you know there is Piute trouble, you shouldn't have pulled a stunt like that!"

Havek was unconcerned. "It's a good thing to have everybody ready. We don't know—maybe the Piutes have sent a party down here. If the white people give them a whipping up north, they'll surely come. The Piutes will have to do something to save their faces."

They were hard put to cover their trail until they came to a very wide and deep lagoon that had once been the main channel of the river. This was called Wild Cow Lagoon. Silently they slipped into the water, and swam with one hand, the other carefully holding their bows high to protect the gut strings. Fortunately the rise in the river had brought the level of the lagoon up so that there was some driftwood floating free. They rounded up three small logs, tied them together with string to make a raft, laid the bows, arrows, and provision sacks across it, and silently pushed it north, swimming as close as possible under the overhanging growth along the bank until they came around a wide bend to the east. There they shoved the raft across to the farther bank, swimming as rapidly as possible without splashing, playing in dead earnest the same game they had been playing for fun since they were small.

At the far side they shoved their raft under the trunk of a cottonwood that had fallen into the water, piled their equipment off on a shelf of mud a foot above the water line, untied the logs, and shoved them cautiously out into the lagoon, one at a time, with a long interval between, so they would float away dry side up and not be suspiciously bunched together.

Then Havek lay down on the cool, dark mud shelf and promptly went to sleep. South Boy saw one log grounded fifty yards below, one floating off north, and the third west, and he said in great content, "It will take more than a frog's nose to follow our trail!"

He felt too good to want to sleep, so he laid the bows and arrows up on the top bank in the dry, hot, half-shade. Then he found a blistering-hot patch of sand in the full sunlight and set the wet ration bags in it to dry. With his back against the bole of a black willow he sat down, just resting, not even thinking, listening a little for possible sounds of a scouting party—hearing nothing but a hundred tiny, harmless noises that drifted through the heat.

Beyond the narrow jungle belt, along the bank and immediately in front of him, was an open patch of salt grass, Jimson weeds, and gourd vines, bounded on its other three sides by large, well grown mesquites. South Boy was listening for sounds behind him, but his eyes were watching that patch of salt grass for no reason at all.

He had sat there a half-hour when the two painted horses came drifting out of the mesquite and began idly browsing off the beans still hanging on the shady side of a tree.

South Boy felt his scalp pull under the half-dry mud pack. He blinked. They were still there. They were painted all right, even though the painted designs were almost invisible under a liberal splattering of mud. There were bits of rags and ribbons tied to their manes and tails. One trailed a broken piece of stake rope that was tied around its neck.

South Boy lay down, rolled to the bank's edge, reached down, and touched Havek's foot. Havek opened his eyes.

"Untie your war arrows," whispered South Boy, and inching along the bank the length of his own body he put his hand on the bow.

Havek, his eyes level with the bank, gave a low chuckle of delight. "Well, did I tell you? You see now, I did a good thing."

Havek laid his arrows up on the bank, took another look at the ponies, jerked the sandals off his feet, thrust them into his hip pocket, and ran straight for the tallest cottonwood and climbed it like a monkey on a stick.

South Boy immediately laid all the arrows in a row, flipped open his big clasp knife, picked up each of the unpointed arrows and resharpened its fire-hardened tip. Then he glanced up to see if Havek was out of sight, pulled out his belly-gun, wiped off the remaining external grease on his overalls, broke it, wiped each cartridge, tore a strip of cloth from his shirt-tail, ran it through the barrel two or three times, reloaded and stuck the gun back into his belt, leaving his shirttail out for easier access. Then he picked up his own bow and seven arrows in his left hand, and Havek's bow and eight arrows—including those with the iron points—in his right hand and ran to the tree.

Havek came sliding down, bug-eyed with excitement, the sweat standing out on his face in great drops. But he shook his head as he stretched out his hand to take his weapons. "No war party close by."

He set out at a slow, cautious trot to circle the horses, cut their back trail, and find out where they came from. He turned west where the first mesquite gave him cover. Then he stopped dead in mid-stride and pointed ahead and to the right with his chin.

There in the soft dust of a gopher's mound was the single track of a moccasined foot. That track removed any possible doubt about the horses. No Indians of the valley ever wore moccasins.

Havek went and squatted over the track, studying it for a scant minute. South Boy, one arrow across his bow and six clutched in his teeth, stood alert, watching, listening. He crouched low and looked around under branches. Havek turned and trotted towards the lagoon, his eyes on the ground. South Boy, satisfied there was nothing bigger than a lizard within two hundred yards, went and looked at the track. A right foot, small and broad. There was a hole worn in the heel of the moccasin. A small-footed, heavy man. From faint tracks in the dust fore and aft, he reckoned the man was short and duck-legged—a horse-Indian, surely. A careless man, to leave such a track in an enemy country.

South Boy turned and trotted after Havek, entering the thicket by an old trail made by the maverick cattle that roamed that part of the valley. There was Havek, standing on the bank looking down at two tracks in the mud at the water's edge.

There the man had knelt down on his right knee to drink. There was a print of the man's right leg, knee to toe. The leg was short and bare but the moccasin top reached almost half-way to the knee!

"Apache!" gasped South Boy through his mouthful of arrows. He had never heard of any other kind of Indian wearing that type of moccasin.

"No. Some kind of Piute," said Havek.

South Boy lingered long enough to satisfy himself of one other thing. The knee print was half full of water that had seeped out on the mud. It was many hours old.

Back in the mesquite, Havek ran his trail like a nosehound, his head down, his eyes strictly on the job of tracking.

South Boy traveled to his left, arrows ready, eyes everywhere but on the trail, ears harking for sounds. Occasionally he would squat, with his eyes level with the ground, and peer ahead.

What was passing through his mind was this: "If we run into the Piutes, they will be asleep under a tree with low branches. If they are all under one tree—fine! We shoot our arrows, very fast. Then we run for the river."

None of this did he attempt to communicate to Havek. Havek would be thinking the same thing.

They would leave fifteen arrow wounds to collect screw-fly maggots. They would be in the brush before a rifle was fired. They would run through brush where no horse could follow. No duck-legged Plateau Indian could hope to catch them afoot —particularly in this heat. When they dived into the swift current of the river they would be in a refuge especially designed for the safety of fish, beavers, and Mojaves. There would be nothing to do but swim with the current and spread the alarm, if indeed Havek's hoax hadn't already aroused the valley.

All together, it promised to be a glorious day.

Havek angled left, and South Boy turned with him. Havek turned right, and South Boy turned at the same instant—like two fish in the same school.

They came to another and smaller salt-grass flat entirely surrounded by mesquite. There in the far side was the remnant of one small fire. Both boys crouched down and spent five minutes looking and listening. Havek got up and went straight across to the ashes. South Boy trotted around the periphery of the clearing. Havek stood spread-legged over the ashes, methodically reading sign. South Boy took the arrows from between his aching jaws and thrust them into the back of his belt. He felt angry and cheated. This was no war party. One lone Piute, a hundred and fifty miles south of where he had any right to be.

Havek beckoned peremptorily and pointed, his nose wrinkled with disgust at the empty shells of two turtles lying in the sand.

South Boy got down on his knees and smelt the ashes. "Yesterday," he said.

"Last night," echoed Havek, and started off again on a trail that led north.

They ran the trail to the north end of the lagoon. There they crossed an old, incoming trail made by the two barefoot ponies. Havek turned back.

They ran this trail to his first camp, near the bank of the river. Here the stranger had eaten two big lizards, a water snake—to the increasing disgust of Havek and South Boy— and a small rabbit. Then he had watered his horses and tied them very carelessly to two mesquite trees, selected because they bore a liberal crop of beans, at least two hundred yards from where he had comfortably bedded himself down in soft dirt.

Why should a "wild" Piute—who, though regarded by the Mojaves as infinitely inferior in strength, speed, and all the cultural matters, was always credited with a great deal of low cunning and vast experience with horses—why should he do such a foolish thing?

Havek and South Boy stared at each other in silent surprise, and went back to reading trail to find the answer.

The Piute's carelessness had cost him his horses.

During the night a mountain lion had twice circled his camp without awakening him, and then stalked the smaller of the horses. It had sprung at her, but she had jumped free, breaking her lead rope. At the same time, the larger horse had jerked out of his rope—South Boy found it tied to the neighboring tree, an oversized neck loop still intact.

The two horses had run off into the brush, the lion running after them in great bounds for about a hundred yards.

The commotion, probably the screams of the mare, had brought the Piute on the run with a firebrand that he threw at the cat.

At the place where he threw it he had jumped up and down many times in fruitless rage—certainly much out of character for a man of the race the Mojaves considered notoriously stolid and emotionless.

And this was not the last of such childish conduct. During the next two days he had stalked the runaways intermittently. Whenever he came in sight of them, he ran after them furiously, and when they outdistanced him, he threw himself on the ground and beat the earth with his hands and feet.

He wasted a great deal of time, too. Much time he squatted in the shade of trees, patting the ground with his hand, evidently singing. More time he spent hunting lizards, turtles, dove squabs, and other nestlings—for he was a gross feeder.

He made many trips to water and slept through the heat of the day. As for arms, he carried a short, thick bow and many arrows, whose imprint lay in the dust at several places. He had no rifle.

In an hour and a half Havek and South Boy ranged the whole territory the Piute had covered in two days of crisscross meandering.

Back at the place where they first crossed his trail, they faced each other and stood nose to nose in exasperated silence. Thirty seconds later Havek exploded. "No man acts like that —ever!"

South Boy said, "All this must have been done to fool somebody. I don't like it." They were oozing sweat and were exhausted; so they returned to the place where they had left their warbags to rest and puzzle over the mystery.

The horses were asleep under the tree where they had first seen them.

South Boy said: "Let them be. They'll stay until the wind rises."

Still playing the game of hide-the-gun, South Boy palmed it cleverly when he stripped and hid it under his clothes. Then he dived into the water and floated a bit, then dived again and swam deep, where it was wonderfully cool. After that he drank, climbed out on the mud shelf, and went to sleep.

An hour later South Boy woke up with a start, and found himself sitting up, listening, his body running with sweat. Not a sound but the rustle of cottonwood leaves, for the gusty afternoon breeze had begun. He thought, Could that Piute have backtracked? He raised his eyes to the level of the bank. The ponies were still lying under the mesquite across the clearing. Not likely they'd lie quiet if they smelt the man who had been chasing them, but South Boy heaved himself up on the bank, took his bow and arrows, and went on a still hunt.

No sign of the enemy. So he came back, took a handful of

mesquite beans from his bag, let himself down into the water where he lay floating, chewing beans, and puzzling over the Piute.

Havek opened his eyes in sleepy inquiry. South Boy shook his head assuringly, then climbed back on the shelf, and went to sleep.

Two hours later, and the sun was low, when he woke up the second time. Havek was sitting on the bank looking down at him. There was excitement and alarm in his eyes.

"That is a crazy man!" he said hotly. "That's why nothing he does is proper."

South Boy sat up. "Bad crazy?"

"Surely, surely," said Havek, switching to Mojave. "Otherwise his people would not have sent him away with two pack-ponies painted like war horses. Look at that mare once!"

South Boy looked over the bank and saw that Havek had caught the Piute's mare, washed her clean of mud and paint, plastered fresh mud over the lion scratch on her ribs and tied her to a willow tree. There she was munching contentedly on some mesquite beans Havek had gathered for her.

"A squaw's pack pony," said South Boy. "I never noticed that when I saw her across the clearing. A Navajo, too."

Navajos had notoriously poor horses. Piutes were always accredited with having good ones. For fifty years they had raided ranches and missions in California, and they made a practice of keeping the biggest and best of their loot and eating the scrubs. Now, fifty years after these raids had ceased, their stock was still good. The Navajos stole their horses in New Mexico where they were poor to start with. They sold or lost the best of them to the Utes, and let the scrubs breed. This mare was potbellied, ewe-necked, and hardly more than thirteen hands high.

The stallion, who was still free, stood half asleep under the cottonwood, a few yards away. He might have been three inches taller, but he was of the same sorry breed.

"A woman's horse, used to being caught by naked children. Naked, I walked right up to her and took hold of the broken rope."

"Stolen from the Navajo for camp work," mused South Boy. "Well—I still don't see why he'd paint 'em up and ride 'em way down here."

"Crazy!" said Havek. "When a man goes crazy his people know that pretty soon nobody will be safe from him. But they tell each other: 'He is our man. We don't want to kill him. Let strangers do it.' So they send him away. Do you remember the San Carlos man?"

South Boy remembered. There had been other roving homicidal maniacs in the recent past, but the San Carlos Apache had left a trail of horror that overshadowed the rest of them. For two weeks every Mojave, every Yavapai, Chemehuevi, Mexican, white man, and hound dog, between the Hassayampa and the Colorado were on the lookout for him. South Boy himself spent almost every daylight hour watching from the top of the tallest tree on the ranch and listening for the cry of alarm to come from up or down the valley. The San Carlos man had killed seven people before he was hunted down, including two wretched women whom he had abducted and then chopped to pieces when they couldn't keep up with the pace he traveled.

South Boy still got sick when he heard the Mojave women detail those killings.

"Rope me that stallion. We better ride," said Havek.

South Boy boosted himself up the bank, picked up the stake rope he had retrieved at the Piute's camp, and bent a honda on the stake end.

So the trail led him from menace to mystery to menace again. Of course, the menace was different now that he knew he had a crazy man to deal with rather than a war party. Now there was no "lift" to it. No exultation, just a sort of horror underneath and a numb anger brought about by the memory of the San Carlos man. The trail was leading him to a kind of varmint hunt. South Boy had the feeling he would rather be hunting a rattlesnake.

The little stallion made a sorry show of snorting and rearing, but there was no real fight in it. Havek came over and took charge of the horse. Havek was obviously nervous and eager to get going, but he wasn't going to ride that horse until he had washed off any possible Piute pollution. He led him away to a low place in the bank.

South Boy got dressed, slipped his head and one shoulder through the string of his war bag, took his bow and arrows, and untied the mare. He didn't bother with any sort of bridle —just looped the broken stake rope around her neck to get it out of the way, jumped onto her back, clamped his knees on her barrel, and whacked her rump with his bow. He figured she'd knee-steer, and she did.

Up-river he went, along the edge of the bank brush, whacking the mare into a lope. The sun was low and the wind was up; the way lay mostly in the half-shade, and the mare went willingly enough. When he came to the Piute's outbound trail, he let her slack down to a running walk.

This ought to be a simple business, he thought. That's a fool's trail. Then he remembered that the San Carlos man had left a fool's trail, but when the hunt grew hot he covered it with superhuman cunning and did such daring, unpredictable, unheard-of things that he had the best trackers in the valley running around in circles, getting nowhere until the cry of alarm brought them to the scene of his next murder.

A few minutes later Havek came pounding up. The stallion was still wet. Havek had tied the free end of the rope to its jaw after the manner of a war-bridle. He tried to take the lead, but the stallion would only follow the mare.

By and by the trail showed the Piute had broken into a trot. Havek pointed down to the widened span between the moccasin track and howled. "See! Here he thought of women.

He is hurrying to get around the head of this lagoon and then double back into the valley and steal a woman!" Thereafter Havek named all the Piute's relatives that might be dead.

South Boy whacked the mare.

When they reached the head of the lagoon they knew, whatever the Piute had on his mind, it wasn't women. The trail led straight ahead, towards Hardyville.

"No, he's thinking about killing White Whiskers!" said South Boy.

White Whiskers was the one remaining inhabitant of the town that had been, before the railroads were built, a river port and the head of steamboat navigation on the Colorado.

South Boy kicked his mare into a run.

White Whiskers was an old man, a very tough, crafty, wise, ingenious old man who had made an oasis in the wilderness singlehanded—but there was no doubt that age had slowed him up. He couldn't run fast or dodge quickly. He would be cold meat for the crazy man's arrows if he didn't happen to have a gun handy.

Ten minutes later the mare ran into the Hardyville clearing at the very head of the Mojave valley, where the river runs out of a cut through the mesa. Up on the mesa rim was a sheet-iron building—an abandoned stamp mill. Down on the flat was a scattering of old adobe walls in various stages of dissolution. Right in the midst of this desolation was White Whiskers' patch of varied green—fig trees, grapevines, melons in square fields, and corn growing in neat rows, around a house and corral with a haystack in it. "A real white man's layout," the Foreman called it. There was an old barge tied up to the river bank. It had once been a ferry. Now it bore a great rattletrap of a water wheel, made from willow poles and lard cans, that revolved with the current and poured an intermittent stream into the high, rickety flume that filled White Whiskers' irrigation ditch.

For once in his life South Boy didn't stop to marvel at the

water wheel. He didn't even see it. There was a man lying stretched out under the biggest fig tree, right by the main ditch. There was a dog beside him.

South Boy's heart jumped. The man had no beard.

The man on the ground was his old friend, the Mormon-hater.

Chapter VIII

THE MORMONHATER

The Mormonhater lay as still as still, flat on his back, one knee up and his head close to the trunk of the tree. The old hound raised his head and looked speculatively at South Boy with deep, sad, bloodshot eyes, but the Mormonhater didn't move. His weather-beaten, sun-wrinkled face was entirely placid, but its normal mahogany color had faded to the sickly hue of new iron rust.

He was dressed in his seldom-worn summer best—a soft white shirt, spotlessly clean, a pair of white duck pants, clean but wrinkled. One leg was rolled up to the knee that was upright. On the lean bare foreleg there was a white bandage stained with dark blood.

Through South Boy's mind ran the lament the Foreman often sang:

> As I was walking the streets of La-redo
> As I was walking in La-redo one day
> I saw a pore cowboy laid out in white linen
> Laid out in white linen, as cold as the clay.

The old hound raised his nose to the sky and bayed dismally, and South Boy buried his head in his hands and sobbed.

Then a voice said, "Shut up, you no-good, stone-deef bastard!" It was the dead man's voice. South Boy uncovered his face, jumped back, and would have run, but he saw the old hound's tail was thumping the ground as he gazed adoringly into the Mormonhater's still face.

"He ain't dead?" South Boy whispered.

"No, but I will be if I don't get kea-weed to make up the blood I lost," said the Mormonhater. "Cook me meat and kea.

If I pass out again, pry my mouth open and make me drink the broth."

South Boy stood shifting his weight from one foot to the other for a few seconds, his mouth full of questions that could hardly wait.

"Kea," croaked the Mormonhater, and South Boy ran to the house for a kettle and meat.

He pulled up to a dead stop on the threshold and peered inside, accustoming his eyes to the semidarkness.

Where was White Whiskers? Maybe he lay dead in there.

As his eyes dilated he saw a blotch of blood in the middle of the adobe floor. The floor had been furrowed and scarred by struggling bodies. Against one wall was a broken chair. Near the door was the long-barreled, single-shot, twenty-two-caliber target pistol that the Mormonhater used to kill trapped animals and small game, likewise broken.

In the farther right-hand corner of the room was a bed. The blanket and the one pillow on it were neither blood-stained nor much disturbed; so the Piute hadn't attacked him in bed, even though the deaf hound had failed to give warning.

The place reeked with chloroform. Near the foot of the bed stood a quart bottle, all covered with bloody finger marks, as was the torn half of an old white shirt from which the Mormonhater had made his bandages. Near by was the gunny sack that held his spare clothes, its contents partly spilled out on the floor.

South Boy stood some thirty seconds, seeing all these things, "reading the story from the sign," after the manner of an Indian: reading how the Mormonhater had jumped out of bed and fought the crazy Piute in the middle of the floor, hitting him with whatever came to his hand. Considering the old trapper's age and size—he was no taller than South Boy and certainly no heavier—and the probable size of the sturdy, duck-legged Indian who made the surprise attack, the Mormonhater had done himself proud.

"A Great Thing," muttered South Boy in awe. "A Great Thing!"

Somehow the Piute had been beaten off. The old man then bandaged his wound, soaked the bandage in chloroform against the ever-present danger of screw-fly blow, dressed himself in his best clothes, in case he should die, and crawled out to the fig tree where there was shade and water.

But what had happened to White Whiskers?

South Boy ran through the room and into the lean-to kitchen rather expecting to find the old nester's body there; but the kitchen was empty and undisturbed. He snatched a kettle from a nail behind the stove, seized a handful of jerky from the meat bin, and ran for the open air, for the house was stifling-hot and the smell of chloroform was sickening.

Out among the grapevines he found the kea—green-leafed, with fleshy blood-red stems—growing rank and knee-high. He wondered if it was the red stems that gave the Mormonhater the idea that it was a blood-builder. No one else gave it that virtue, though both Mojaves and whites ate it occasionally.

"One thing I do know. White Whiskers ain't here, and it's a cinch he ain't been for some time, or these weeds wouldn't be this big." White Whiskers was a careful cultivator. The Mormonhater wasn't. He cherished the notion, common among northern Indians but foreign to Mojave thinking, that field work was women's work.

South Boy ran back to the fig tree, fetched wood, and built his cook fire by the ditch. The Mormonhater hadn't moved. He saw now that there were bruises on his chest. His color was ghastly.

South Boy began feeling alone and afraid again. No leg wound would make him look that sick, he thought. What else is under his shirt besides those bruises? Maybe it hides a belly wound that doesn't bleed? He was feeling very much Indian and began to shiver with the panic that besets an Indian when he finds himself all alone with the dead. He wanted to howl, but wanted a friend to howl with him. Then he wanted to run. Then he saw the hound lying still by the old man, snoring peacefully, and somehow that quieted him.

He knew, though, that he must find something to do while he waited for the pot to boil, or thoughts might come out of the back of his head and drive him wild. Remembering his gun and the numerous wettings it had received, he went around to the tool-shed back of the house and found a can of skunk grease—the Mormonhater's sovereign lubricant. He wiped and greased the gun and each of the cartridges, shook the cartridges dubiously, tried the action of the gun, greased it again and thrust it back into his pants.

The kettle was just beginning to simmer. The Mormonhater lay as he had lain without visible or audible signs of life, and the hound snored mightily. The sun had gone down into Nevada. South Boy, eager to keep busy, remembered the lion scratch on the mare's ribs.

He ran to the house, found a box of pine tar in the kitchen and with that and the bloodstained bottle from the foot of the bed he went through the grapevines to the hayfield where the horses were grazing in a good stand of volunteer, second-crop oats that was just yellowing. The mare made little objection when he led her to the ditch and washed the mud out of the scratch and looked diligently for screw-fly larvae.

The screw fly lays her eggs only in fresh, bleeding wounds, for her maggots thrive only in sound, living flesh. There were none in the scratch that he could see, but South Boy said to himself, "I'll take no chances in this kind of weather," and uncorked the bottle of chloroform.

He got a whiff of it before he poured it into the wound. It smelled strong. It smelled stronger yet when he sloshed it over the scratch. After that he had his hands full, for the sting of the medicine suddenly turned the mare into a kicking, biting fury. He hung onto the rope and let her fight it out, little realizing that he had aroused in her the dogged mustang hate that was to cause him so much trouble the next day. He just clung to the rope until he could pull her head around and slap a protective gob of tar over the scratch.

"Damn!" he said when he got another overpowering whiff as he corked the bottle. "That's no one-in-five solution. That's the pure quill!"

He walked back to the fire in the last of the short twilight. A strong, steady breeze had sprung up from the south, and the old hound was sitting up exploring it with his nose. South Boy stopped in his tracks and began swearing to himself, slowly and bitterly, after the manner of the Foreman.

"The damn chloroform! That's why he looks so sick."

He went over and shook the Mormonhater none too gently. "Hey! Wake up!"

"Where's the kea?" asked the old man.

"Wait till it's ready. Say, why didn't you dilute that chloroform? You oughta know the pure stuff would make you sick when you slapped it around so free."

"Look," said the Mormonhater. "I was bleeding to death. I never had a leg bleed so bad in my life. I had to get it bandaged and doctored in a hurry. Anyhow that bottle belongs to White Whiskers. How in hell was I to know how strong it was? Where's that kea? I want my blood built back."

South Boy gave a long slow "Ca-a-a-aw!" expressive of infinite disgust, and went slowly towards the house to fetch eating tools. He had worked himself into a high pitch of pity and horror over the old man, and now he felt badly let down. "Chloroform-sick," he said. "A lot of fuss over nothing."

"See if that son of a bitch got away with my new Winchester," the Mormonhater called after him. "I forgot to look."

South Boy came back with the Winchester under his arm and cups and tin plates in his hands. "It was down on the floor behind the bed," he said, and handed the rifle to the old man.

"Yeh. It wasn't in the corner when I reached for it. Must

have slipped down." He jacked open the chamber, felt to see if it was loaded, then lovingly laid the weapon across his lap.

"Seems like you was mighty careless," said South Boy, morosely picking his sometime hero to pieces. "The Piute got away with the old Springfield and your bullet bag. They ain't in there any place."

The Mormonhater nodded complacently. "Yeh. They was right by the door. He must have snatched them up when he ran out—after the old dog woke up and took hold of him."

"That's swell! Havek's out there trailing him alone. He won't be looking for him to have no rifle, because the sign back there in the flat didn't read no rifle. He'll get bush-whacked, sure!"

The Mormonhater said: "Ease your mind and get me some kea. The boy's all right."

South Boy scratched at the rash that heat and sweat had raised on his back and belly, his brooding eyes on the northern horizon over which played a fitful light. There was a light-ning storm up there, below the curve of the world and too far away for the sound of the thunder to carry. "I'd have been up there with him, but I thought you was real bad hurt." And he dipped up a cup of broth and kea.

The Mormonhater took the cup and sipped eagerly. "Good! I can feel my blood building up already."

"It's Havek's blood that's bothering me," said South Boy. He dipped himself out a plateful of meat and greens and sat glowering—waiting for it to get cool enough for his fingers. "I'd worry worse, but I think small of this Piute. Knifing a man in the leg. That's a silly business."

"Don't think he wasn't trying to do better!" said the Mor-monhater with some heat. "I just moved too fast for him."

South Boy began eating. The meat and greens tasted good, but they burnt his mouth. The world seemed very black, for the fire had died down to a bed of ash-covered coals and there was no moon yet. The stars were few and pale, giving less light than the flickering glow in the north. The breeze came in hot, fitful gusts. The creak and groan of the water wheel was a wail of pain and a cry of warning, and the talk of the big river was uneasy, quarrelsome, alarming. Even the chatter of the ditchwater was nerve-rasping.

"How do you know Havek will be back?" South Boy insisted, his belligerency rising.

Instead of answering, the Mormonhater gave vent to a flood of scurrilous invectives against the absent White Whiskers and launched into the tale of how it happened that this hard-working stay-at-home had been gone all summer. South Boy listened in spite of anxiety, impatience, and anger, for the Mormonhater was a skillful story-teller.

He told in full detail how he had brought his boat up-river just before the June flood to take White Whiskers on their annual wild-beef hunt. As soon as the river flooded the bottom land, driving the wild cattle into a limited area of higher ground east of Wild Cow lagoon, the two of them rowed over there and killed enough beef for their year's supply of jerky. And while they were drying the meat, White Whiskers remembered that he hadn't eaten venison in years.

The nearest deer hunting that was accessible by boat was two hundred miles downstream at Moon Mountain Slough, and the Mormonhater refused to make any such journey in hot weather. But in a moment of weakness he did loan White Whiskers his boat and his two younger dogs with the strict understanding that White Whiskers was to come back in July, when the flood subsided and the coming of intermittent south winds would fill the boat's tarpaulin sail and make up-river navigation possible.

"And here it is two days short of September, and I'm still stuck here, working my fingers to the bone taking care of his damn truck patch," the old man concluded.

South Boy said: "Yeh. From the size of the weeds you must have been working yourself to death. And listen to the water wheel! Didn't you ever try greasing it?"

The Mormonhater paid no heed to him but went on blackguarding White Whiskers. "He's probably laying up with some Mexican squaw in Ehrenburg."

"He's probably laying up alongside the bank some place waiting for a south wind. There ain't been a good south wind all this summer, and you know it," said South Boy.

The Mormonhater said nothing for a long time. Then he began cursing again. This time he was cursing himself. "Damn me for a muttonhead! I had three chances to kill him and didn't!"

"White Whiskers!" cried South Boy, aghast and furious.

"No, you idjit. The Piute. But if I did kill him I'd have had to bury him, and it was just too damn hot."

He launched into another story. How, at dusk, three days before, the Piute had appeared at the edge of the clearing riding one painted pony and leading the other. The Mormonhater was sitting in the doorway of the house, the old Springfield across his knees, for he'd heard a coyote in the brush. He still used the Springfield against such varmints because its reload cartridges cost much less than store-bought ammunition for the Winchester.

The Piute gazed at the rifle with eager eyes and offered, in passable Spanish, to trade a horse for it.

The Mormonhater rejected the offer in the Piute's own tongue. Whereupon the Piute retreated into the brush and began screaming that he was going to the Chemehuevi with his medicine horses to lead them in a general massacre of the Mojaves and the whites.

"I could have got him easy, but I figgered that the Chemehuevis would knock him on the head and throw him into the river for his crazy talk."

"He never got to the Chemehuevi," said South Boy, watching the flickering lights in the north and worrying about Havek.

The old man nodded. "I know. Yesterday I saw him scouting around afoot. I had a couple of more chances to down him, but it was still too hot for grave-digging. I figgered the dog and me could keep him off. I didn't know the dog had got so deef. I didn't know another thing I know now: the smell of that Piute, and the words he said when the dog finally did take hold of him."

The Mormonhater looked very solemn, as though what he said was very important; but he failed to impress South Boy, who said petulantly: "Havek trails too close. He's easy meat for a bushwhacker. I oughta high-tail up there and see what's happened to him."

"Quit worryin' about the Mojave," said the Mormonhater. "He'll be here."

"He'll be here! He'll be here!" South Boy mocked savagely. "When? How soon? And how in hell do you know, anyway?"

"The sign says it."

South Boy stood up trying to see the old man's face, but it was nearly pitch-dark under the tree. So he went and moved the kettle to one side and put two sticks on the embers. When they had blazed enough to give considerable light he walked back and again tried to see what was on the upturned face, but the fire cast heavy, restless, uncertain lights and shadows across it.

"What sign?" he asked.

"Nothing you can read," said the Mormonhater.

"All right," said South Boy. "From what sign *should* I read that Havek's riding back? Name it, and tell me where I miss seeing it."

The Mormonhater wouldn't answer, and when South Boy kept insisting he made the buzzing sound down in his throat that an old Indian makes when he doesn't want to answer a question.

If the old man had been an Indian, South Boy would have said nothing more; but the Mormonhater was supposed to be a white man, and so South Boy, peevish from the heat, from worry, and from a long, hard day, insisted on a logical answer. Getting none at all, he finally said: "Tell me. Are you a far-seer—like some Mojave old man? If you are, I won't ask anything more about it. But if you are reading sign that I should see I want to know!"

The Mormonhater just looked up into the fig tree.

The hair on the back of South Boy's neck prickled with anger. He always makes me mad when he gets like this, he told himself; but he hung onto his temper for the time being and remained silent.

Then the Mormonhater said with slow emphasis, "That Piute had the smell of a witch about him." He used the word "witch" to indicate a sorcerer of either sex, as an Indian does when he speaks English.

South Boy pulled his knees up under his chin and waited for three or four sullen minutes before he said, "Crazy people won't wash; so they smell bad."

"A witch, and the worst kind of a witch," said the old man. "For a he-witch is worse than a she-witch, and a Piute witch is worse than any other kind, worse even than a Zuñi. He spoke a curse and a warning when he ran away last night. He said he had the power of world-blasting."

South Boy said, "Caw!" derisively.

The Mormonhater gave him a hard look. "Go over to the south side of the house and you'll find a long screw-bean stick that White Whiskers has been saving for a hoe handle. Fetch it. I want to walk about a bit."

South Boy got up and went to get the stick, saying sullenly, "You try using a stick on me, and you sure as hell won't prosper." The Mormonhater had used a stick on him before, but that was in a good cause and South Boy never resented it.

When he came back the Mormonhater took the stick, hopped

over to the kettle and drank a dipperful of broth, and hopped back and sat down. "You should listen and learn, because you might need to know." He leaned back and looked up, as though he might be earnestly contemplating some star shining through a gap in the fig leaves. "Now you, being white-raised and Mojave-raised, don't know nothing about witches. You probably think they are something like 'Mojave doctors.' That's not so, at all.

"A witch and a doctor, they're different things. A doctor ain't bad, not to start with. His powers is like dynamite or whisky. They're bad only when they're used bad. Sometimes a doctor goes sour on the world, and he uses his powers to kill people or to make floods instead of curing people or making good rains. But a witch's powers is bad to start with. They're for death and destruction, and nothing else.

"Them that use them are to be destroyed!" he emphasized each of those words by a thump on the ground with his stick.

South Boy said, "Caw!" again. "Witches is poor-trash business." To him witches pertained to inferior people—foreign Indians, Mexicans, poor whites, and negroes. People of consequence, either white or Mojave, didn't believe in them or had no truck with them.

"That's right," said the Mormonhater. "Only the poor, the trod-on, the half-starved, the desperate, and the crazy take to witching. But that don't make them less dangerous because it's them kind that want vengeance against the whole world. The Piutes have so many witches because the other Indians shoved them back into the desert where they had to eat lizards and crickets and bush rats and weed tops or starve. When the Spaniards came to New Mexico living got a little bit easier for the Piutes because they learned to steal each other's children and trade them to the Spaniards for horses. Then the Spaniards came to California, which was closer, and the Piutes learned to steal horses and lived pretty good.

"Then the Americans came and stopped the horse stealing

and the slave trading, and they was shoved back some more and trod on some more, and starved some more.

"Now you take this man: I can tell by his talk that he comes from the little bunch of Piutes that has always wandered around among the Navajo like gypsies do among white people, picking up a living the best they can. I tell by his talk he was a lone traveler for some time, visiting many tribes. I think he was a Ghost Dance messenger, for many Piutes carried the Ghost Dance religion out among the tribes about ten-fifteen years back.

"Ghost dancing was supposed to bring all the dead Indians back to life. All it did was to get a lot more Indians killed. I think when ghost dancing failed, this Piute went crazy and took up witching. Must have picked up with an old Hopi witch woman sometime, because he used a Hopi witching curse among the rest." The Mormonhater stopped for breath.

"What I want to know is, are you a farseer or not?" said South Boy.

"What you need to know is that when the dog took hold of the Piute his liver turned green, and he ran away to make world's-end medicine. That's why he's got to be killed!"

"Will you give me an answer? Are you a farseer?"

"Well, if I was, would I tell you!" roared the old man.

"I can't ease my mind about Havek till I know for sure whether you're farseeing him coming here, or just guessing."

The Mormonhater began cursing in English, loudly at first. Then the strength of his voice diminished until it was no more than a whisper. "But you got to pay heed to me." It was a plea rather than a command. "The Piute is a witch, and he has world's end in his heart and he must be destroyed, like it says in the Bible. He got away with my Bible, too. It's in the bullet bag. I want to get it back. There is certain medicine I must make."

South Boy began laughing without mirth. "You're a great one to talk about what it says in the Bible. 'What does it say

Tom Paine's book, or Bob Ingersoll's?' You up and tell me. My mother is ruining my mind by filling me full of Bible superstition and you give me Ingersoll to read and now you tell me to believe the most superstitious thing in the Bible. You're *ohiva-michiva*," he accused—which was schoolboy slang for flighty, inconsistent person, and a very bad thing to call a man.

The Mormonhater barked, "Mind your tongue!"

By this time South Boy's temper had stewed too long in the heat, and it broke into a boil.

"You harp about me being fed on Bible superstition, and then last year, when there was that earthquake, what did you do? You ran your boat up to the head of Mesquite Slough, and there you stayed two weeks, yelling and preaching and Bible-reading. You thought there weren't nobody but your dogs to hear you, but Mojaves lay in the brush and listened and told me about it."

The Mormonhater said nothing and kept his face so hidden in the shadow that South Boy couldn't even have the satisfaction of knowing how angry he was.

"Cohiva-michiva," he said again. "One thing one time, another thing another time." And he picked up his bow and arrows and walked out into the darkness, nursing his anger and thinking of the many ways in which the Mormonhater had proven himself to be an inconsistent person.

The Mormonhater prided himself on telling the truth. He said his word was good from the Yaqui country to the Big Canyons, and his word *was good* in most matters. But about his own birth and early life he was as full of lies as a melon is full of seeds. He said that he was one of the children who survived the Mountain Meadow massacre up by the headwaters of the Virgin River in 1857. He also claimed that he had raided the Mission San Luis Obispo with Pegleg Smith on the memorable occasion when Pegleg and his thirty-six Shoshone brothers-in-law stole three thousand horses. As the oldest of the Mountain Meadow survivors was no more than four or five and the San Luis Obispo raid took place some twenty years before the massacre, the Mormonhater was convicted of lying by his own mouth.

Likewise the Mormonhater prided himself on being a reasonable man who would listen to any and all sides of a question and weigh all arguments for the truth they might have. And this was true enough on any subject on which his prejudices were not aroused. He was the best wolfer and coyote trapper in the Southwest; yet he would listen to anybody's theory on the habits of a coyote, no matter how outlandish and full of obvious errors it might be, for he said, "I kin never know so much but what some fool might teach me a little more."

But if a man made an obviously true statement that touched one of his prejudices, such as, "The Mormons are good farmers—wherever they settle, they make the desert bloom," the Mormonhater would fly into a rage and stomp away sputtering obscenities. If he brought up the subject of the Mormons himself, he invariably began making wild, ludicrous statements. One was: "Mormons never go barefoot. They don't want people to see they got goats' hoofs."

He said that once to a crowd of idlers in front of Monnehan and Murphy's store in Needles. Whereupon an indignant stranger removed both shoes from large, normal feet and said he was a Mormon and the son of a Mormon, and he was going to prove his feet were good, solid, human flesh by kicking a dirty liar's butt up over his belt.

The Mormonhater ran. He ran to the river just two jumps ahead of the stranger's big feet, leaped into his boat, and shoved off; and for a year afterward he never appeared in Needles.

Strange to say, although he had proven his strength and courage many times and although he swore that his life was devoted to a perpetual feud against all Mormons, he ran away every time one of them confronted him. The man who ran him out of Needles said that this was because the trapper was a Jack-Mormon, an apostate who had come to hate his own kind but couldn't make himself raise a hand against one of them.

Cohiva-michiva, surely, thought South Boy. He had wandered north up the trail until he found a saw-cut cottonwood stump by a building with one wall still standing, and he sat there wiping sweat from his face and scratching himself until his annoyance slowly oozed away.

By and by he remembered that the Mormonhater had always been a generous friend and a wise teacher.

True, his teaching methods were not exactly in accord with modern pedagogy. He taught South Boy to shoot with the old Springfield, a number of tin cans, and a willow switch. The cans had a large red tomato in the center of each label. If South Boy shot high, the switch would cut across his legs with a stinging crack and the Mormonhater would shriek: "Notch it! Notch it, you blind idjit! You got to see a *leetle* of that foresight!" If he shot to the right or the left the old man would slash at his legs with extra fury. "Damn your sunken, coal-black soul! Hold that gun squa-are! Are you trying to miss?"

When he did hit the tomato, the stick didn't fall. The Mormonhater only muttered, "That's something like it!" And when he hit three tomatoes in a row, the old man fished in his pocket and produced a shiny dime—probably the only coin he had in the world, for he seldom had any money. His business with the traders, in hides, furs, wild honey, and placer gold—gleaned color by color from old worn-out diggings—was conducted almost entirely on the barter basis.

"Buy yourself a short-bit's worth of toothache the next time you go to the Fort," he said, in way of reward.

The effectiveness of this method was proven by the fact

that South Boy shot with the grown men at the last Fourth of July matches.

The Mormonhater was clean in his personal habits, in spite of the fact that more than half the year he lived in a greasy old flat-bottom rowboat with three dogs, rusty traps, bilge water, stinking hides, bottles and cans of skunk grease and snake oil, and all the bloody refuse of killing and skinning. He was clean in his mind, too, although on occasions his mouth would spout obscenities as carelessly and unconsciously as the little geysers of the Salton Sink spout mud.

It occurred to South Boy that it was the nature of all white men to be inconsistent. He had heard that from the Indians many times.

Take the Foreman, for instance. On rare occasions, usually when he was drunk, he was all roaring good humor, the funniest, jolliest man in Arizona. Then for days he'd either be full of whining, complaining curses or sullen, dangerous silence. When he was in the latter mood, nobody dared to speak to him except South Boy's father, who was just as big as the Foreman, and just as gloomy, and never feared anybody or anything.

There were days when the Foreman would devote hours of his time, patiently and without hope or desire of reward, to teaching South Boy "what's needed to make a good man." In fact he was more patient than the Mormonhater, more given to careful, if somewhat long-winded, explanations—and he never used a switch. Whether it was fighting, rope handling, colt breaking, trail driving, or packing, he drilled South Boy until he was letter-perfect in theory and sufficiently able in practice, without losing his temper or raising his voice.

Then there were days when he would not speak to the boy at all and glared murderously out of cold gray eyes when spoken to. Again he would start to rave out of all reason, cursing Fate for dealing him "three dirty deuces from the bottom of the deck": a Mexican hay bag for a wife, a life in exile, and a thirst for hard liquor.

The moon came up angry and red and paled the flickering in the north until it was hardly visible. His mind still in a ferment, South Boy was thinking that there was one great difference between the Foreman and the Mormonhater. Drunk, sober, laughing or sullen, kind or murderous, the Foreman was always the Foreman; but the Mormonhater—when he talked Mojave he *was* Mojave in thought and gesture, when he talked Chemehuevi he was Chemehuevi, and when he talked Mexican he was Mexican. When he preached Tom Paine and Bob Ingersoll, he was a freethinker, and when he got one of his religious streaks he was a back-country exhorter full of zeal and the fear of hell fire.

"It is he who is cohiva-michiva indeed. He is too many men," said South Boy. Then the thought came to him: "How many men am I? How many times have I changed from thinking Mojave to thinking white this past day? What am I but cohiva-michiva myself?" And he began feeling very scared and humble, for his anger had burnt itself out, leaving him weak, sweat-sodden and very miserable.

Just when he had dropped to the very depth of misery there came a far sound, muffled by the hot, thick air. He stood up on the stump to listen. It came louder and louder and his heart began beating fast, for it was a strong, full voice, still far off, singing "The Ravens."

Chapter IX

BATTLE TELLING

Havek rode out of the moonlight into the shadow by the tree with his bow across his back, his arrows in his belt and a three-foot piece of mesquite wood about as thick as a man's arm swinging in his hand. He slid off his horse, laid his bow and arrows on the ground, sat down, pulled his big clasp knife out of his pocket, and immediately set to work whittling on the mesquite stick.

"So you left him alive!" said the Mormonhater in disgust.

Havek said nothing. South Boy, who ran at the horse's head, slipped the war bridle off its jaw and bent the rope around its neck. The horse had been a-lather, but it was dry now. So Havek had ridden hard up-river and then come back slowly.

"Where is he?" asked the Mormonhater sharply.

Havek raised his head and pointed north with his chin. He went on whittling at the mesquite stick as though his life depended upon it.

"God damn this leg!" said the Mormonhater. "I should go and tend to him myself." After that he said nothing, but watched Havek with keen speculation.

South Boy led Havek's horse through the grapevines and then turned him loose and watched him go nickering off to join the mare in the hayfield. He went to the kettle and dished out a plate of meat and greens and set it by Havek, who paid no attention to it. He was whittling with fury and a kind of exultation. South Boy took one look at what he was doing, picked up his bow and arrows, and trotted off across the field to the ruined houses, where he stirred in an old rubbish heap two or three times with his bow to scare out any sidewinder, scorpion, black-widow spider, or other night varmint, then picked up several pieces of bottle glass and trotted back to the fire with them. There he sat opposite Havek and waited, wide-eyed with excitement.

Havek had already roughed out a club that was something like a ball bat. South Boy picked out a piece of glass with a good sharp edge. In two or three minutes Havek suddenly thrust the club at South Boy. He seized it and immediately scraped off long, thin shavings. Havek's hand dipped into the plate and shoved a dripping handful of its contents into his mouth.

"We won't get a word out of him now," said the Mormon-hater.

"What's the need?" asked South Boy. "You know what happened. If you don't, I'll tell you. Havek trailed the Piute fast-like until the trail got hot. Then he trailed him slow and cautious-like. Then he found the place where he stopped. Then he scouted all around. Then he came back slow-like. He said to himself: 'I'll make me a club. Tomorrow I'll do a Great Thing when South Boy's there to see it.' "

South Boy looked at Havek, and Havek gulped and nodded.

The old man said: "I could have told you that, and I'll tell you some more. The Piute made his camp by a pile of last year's driftwood near where a thick crop of this year's willows covers the whole sand bar from the foot of the cliff to the river. Ain't it so?"

Havek looked owl-eyed with surprise.

"But what I want to know—has he laid a small fire on a flat rock, and what does his medicine bag look like?"

Havek shook his head. He picked up a piece of glass and reached for his club.

"Yah!" spat the Mormonhater. "You don't know. And you lay there on top of the driftwood and looked right at him. Why didn't you shoot him while you had the chance? That's Mojave silliness for you. There's a man that may be the death of us all, but you let him live because you got your mind set on makin' a show. It's like a man who sees a great big snake. He's got a gun on him, but he don't use it. He says, 'Wait till I gather the neighbors, then I'll make a big hero of myself by killin' you with a little stick.' "

"That's a white man talking," said South Boy in Mojave.

There was a long spell of stifling silence, punctuated by the scraping of wood, the murmur of the water in the ditch, the talk of the river, and the squeak and splash of the water wheel, all of which were cheerful sounds, now.

The Mormonhater said, "Oh, Lord, how can I make these fools listen?"

He began singing to himself in a language South Boy could not understand. Neither South Boy nor Havek paid it much attention, for they were absorbed with the sight and feel of the club that was taking shape under their hands.

By and by the old man stopped singing, and Havek began chanting a song of his own:

> "I'll strike this way—
> I'll strike that way—
> I'll break his skull—
> I'll scatter his brains."

South Boy couldn't sing, so he provided a loud grunt at the end of each line, by way of refrain. He felt fine; his hands were busy, wiping the sweat from his face, or feeling over the club for rough spots, or scraping, or putting wood on the fire to make more light, or dipping water from the ditch to drink or pour over himself or Havek.

All the while the Mormonhater sat quietly and said nothing. Then when Havek's song had about worn itself out, he said, "Listen—listen!" in a high voice and began speaking in Mojave in the style and manner of an old man who recites a Great Telling while young men work. He said:

"In the years after the Mojave lost many dead in the Pima

country, after they had killed the white travelers, after they took the cattle, the soldiers came to the valley and rifle balls ripped up the ranks of the clubbers. The soldiers charged the clubbers with their bayonets, and half of all the big men died.

"So then the soldiers made the Fort right in the middle of the Mojave country. There was peace. The Mojaves said, 'This is the end of the world for us,' and they cried four years. The old men said: 'The old way of fighting that made the Mojaves feared from the Rio Grande to the Ocean is no good any more. Nothing that has been good since the First Times is good now.'

"So it was that a man from Shivwits was able to come down-river and set himself up as a doctor on Cottonwood Island, where the Mojaves had two or three rancherias in those days. And the Mojaves took their sick up-river for him to sing over, for in the bitterness of their defeat they held themselves so cheap that they thought even a despised Piute was better than a doctor of their own.

"For two years the Piute did well. Then a woman he sang over died from delayed childbirth. And the woman's brothers said: 'We'd kill a doctor of our own for such a matter. Let's kill this Piute.' And they did.

"Now in the days before the soldiers came the Piutes would have done nothing. But now they knew that half of the Big Men were dead. So the Shivwits sent to the Kaibab and the Paviosto and one or two more Piute bands and said: 'We've got rifles and we've got horses. We can kill Mojaves just like the soldiers did.' And they came down-river to Cottonwood Island and they killed some Mojave women."

At this place South Boy asked Havek, "Is this a true telling?"

Havek wiped the sweat out of his eyes and said: "Surely. Surely. I heard it before. No old man of The People ever told it better."

The Mormonhater went on. "In the old days the clubbers would have started north before the woman's ashes were cold, but now the old men held a council and talked for four days.

Some wanted to go. Others said, 'If we go to war the soldier will be offended, and they will kill us.' Others said: 'The Piute have been trading horses for rifles lately. Every Piute has a good rifle, and we have none. Clubs can't defeat these new kinds of guns. We know that.'

"So the old men talked and did nothing.

"But while they talked some of the young men—boys who would have carried straight clubs, like that one, and fough in the rear rank behind the big men—they made their own talk They said, 'The big men won't fight. We'll make this a small men war. We'll fight it our own way. Thick bush will b our friend. Darkness will blind bullets. Rough rocks will stop horses. We will fight after the manner of Apaches. So let' make Apache arrows and go up-river.'

"So the small-men war began. Four young men, who were at the right age to go name-traveling, set out for the Piute country with Apaches' arrows and small-men clubs, and when they came back they said their names were Kill-three, Kill-two, Piute-bleeds, and Wolf-in-the-Brush. The old men were angry and refused to honor such names. They said: 'You are no better than Apaches or Diggers or coyotes. Any coward can kill and run.'

"But the women and the young men feasted them through the camp, and after that, instead of running naked, a young man took iron arrows with him when he went name-traveling and went up to harry the Piutes, although the old men said 'This kind of business will bring neither honor to us nor fear to the enemy. Any kind of war is useless unless it does those two things.'

"As for the Piutes they said: 'What have we to fear? The Mojaves don't fight like Mojaves any more. They fight like ordinary Indians. Once they were grizzly bears. Now they are little foxes. Let us go down to Cottonwood Island and kill everybody.'

"When the Piutes came down the river this time, Irataba

the Great Traveler, the chief of all the Mojaves, was visiting up there on Cottonwood Island. He was a great man. The year before, he had been all the way to Washington by steamboat and by railroad train. He had lived in the White House with President Lincoln for seven days, and he was wearing the army general's uniform the President had given him. All the Mojaves had seen it except the people on Cottonwood, who lived so far away from everybody. That's why he went up there.

"A boy came down-river crying, 'One hundred Piutes are coming!' Irataba said: 'Let the men follow me. I'll go meet them. Let the women stay and burn all the crops and granaries and then go down-river for help.'

"With arrows and a few old shotguns they met the Piutes and fought them from willow thicket to willow thicket, retreating gradually back to Cottonwood Island. Then Irataba found that the women had run away without destroying all the crops. So he told his men to take to the river while he stayed to finish the burning.

"And there the Piutes caught him. They were afraid to kill him while he wore the soldier's uniform, so they set about to strip him. But when they had stripped him, they couldn't hold him. He threw them off and jumped into the river. And the Piutes were afraid he'd bring back the soldiers, so they ran up-river.

"The Mojaves talked again, but nothing was decided and nothing was done. The small-men raids went on, and they accomplished nothing. At last some boy killed a Paviosto chief. So the Piute bands all got together and they sent a real army down-river. That was five years after the stripping of Irataba."

At this point the Mormonhater started beating the ground with his stick to give emphasis to his words.

"I was here. I saw them come. I drove my mules in here to Hardyville. I looked up the river trail up there." He turned around and pointed up above the old stamp mill, using his hand

and his chin both, Indian-fashion. "I ran my mules down the street. I cried out. Every door closed. Every door bar fell. Every window showed a rifle muzzle. But the Piutes only came as far as the edge of the mesa and cried, 'Peace, peace! Our war is with the Mojaves!' and they ran along the rim of the mesa, their shirttails flapping in the wind, their rifle butts trailing, for they had come by the river and left their horses behind.

"I went to my house. I was married then to a Mojave of the Chacha clan. She was gone. I went out into the mesquite looking for her, and there, right over there, I found the tracks of many running women. Every white man's wife had run to tell her people."

The Mormonhater dropped his stick and began pounding his left hand with his right fist. "South I ran on my woman's trail. Then I heard the long yell—old men yelling from the housetops.

"The Piutes came down off the mesa. They spread out across the playa, their right flank skirted the willows. Out of the willows the Mojaves shot arrows and killed one man. I was there. I saw it. The Piutes lay down on their bellies and shot into the willows. The Mojaves were only twenty, but they yelled like a hundred. They lay close to the ground and screamed and sang their death songs. So the Piutes charged the willows, and the Mojaves ran away to the next thicket.

"There the Mojaves had a hundred young men lying in ambush and they killed five Piutes. The rest of the Piutes ran back to the mesa yelling, 'Where are the Mojaves that used to fight in the open?'

"I ran down to the Fort, and there was Yellow Road; and he had a hundred big-men clubbers with him, and he had a hundred small men behind him, and he was telling the major: 'These people up there, they think the Mojaves have turned into coyotes, otherwise they wouldn't dare come into this valley. Now you stay out of this fight. You stand on the mesa and watch us. Let everybody come and watch us, for you'll see something you'll never see again.'

"So I went with the soldiers and the traders and the white women, and we stood on a rise of ground and we watched the Mojaves run slowly across the mesa, the big men, the face smashers, stretched out in a long line, the small men, the skull crackers, running behind them. Thus the Mojaves returned to the First Times that day.

"There was a sand hill over on the mesa. On top of the sand hill were the Piutes, waiting.

"Now the major had a big gold watch. When the clubbers came to the foot of the hill, he pulled the watch out of his pocket and began counting off the minutes. When he counted 'One!' the feet of the clubbers were already in the sand. The Piutes fired one volley and five in the front ranks of the Mojaves fell down. The rest went on, five yards apart, bent low, running with short steps, big feet making sand fly. The Piutes yelled. They were all shooting. Some had repeating rifles, they shot too fast. Some had muzzle loaders, they shot too slow.

"The major called 'Two!' The first clubber reached the top of the hill. His hand reached out for the first Piute. His club smashed up into the Piute's face. I was there. I saw it. The Piute came sailing over the Mojave's head. He hit the slope of the sand hill and came sliding down pushing the sand before him. Then he slid down by the second rank of Mojaves and a boy with a straight bat reached out and broke his head as he slid on by.

"Then the top of the hill was hidden in flying sand. I could see nothing, but the shots were few and the yells were Mojave yells. Then I saw Yellow Road standing out in a cloud of sand waving a shirt to show the battle was won and the Piutes were running.

"The major looked at his watch and called out, 'Three!' "

The Mormonhater stopped his telling. Nobody said anything for a minute. Then Havek suddenly hurled his club into the air, gave a short high scream of triumph, like the squall of a fox. He caught the club as it came down, and, laying it on the ground, he lay down beside it, stretched out like a man who is utterly exhausted, and immediately went to sleep.

"Well, damn my liver and lights!" said the Mormonhater. "I should have knowed that would happen." And he began cursing in a bitter monotone.

"What happened?" asked South Boy.

"What happened? Why, you blind idjit, he went to sleep on me!"

"I mean, What happened after the battle?"

"Oh, the soldiers give the Mojaves a big feed of government beef and— Hey, you lay down there and git to sleep, too! I ain't going to waste any breath on you. I wanted to get the Mojave boy's attention so's I could tell him how to deal with the witch—and he up and went to sleep on me. Well, let it go till morning. And you—you sleep! If'n I see I can't depend on him, I'll have to depend on you to keep the world together in the morning.

"Damn this leg!" he went on. "It gripes my guts to have to trust this business to a couple of boys."

South Boy lay down and went to sleep not because he wanted to, or because the Mormonhater told him to, but because he was so tired that he could not sit up any longer.

Chapter X

THE PIUTE

HE AWOKE suddenly. The Mormonhater's stick was rapping a vigorous tattoo on his backside. South Boy cried out angrily and struck at the stick with his hands. The Mormonhater said, "Here, drink this," and gave him a cup of hot coffee.

He was about to protest that he'd had no sleep when he saw that the moon was already over Nevada. So four hours had gone by, and morning was coming. He shook the sleep out of his eyes and downed the strong coffee. The sweat broke out all over him.

"Fetch them horses, and shake it up," said the Mormonhater.

South Boy heaved himself to his feet, stumbled over Havek's inert body and headed for the river.

The air seemed to press down upon him. It stank, and it had weight. He seemed to move heavily against it. It was jungle air, damp and steaming, that had been slowly coming up the Gulf of California and into the valley. South Boy knew that such air only came with the very worst of crazy weather.

The river was so cold the shock of it took his breath. Then he climbed out and pulled on his clothes. Up by the barge that held the complaining water wheel he found the horses. They had just finished drinking. South Boy picked up the lead rope of the mare and approached her to tie a war bridle on her jaw. She laid her ears back and rolled the whites of her eyes and lashed at him with her teeth.

"Damn you, what do you have to go mean for? I had to doctor you or the screw worms would eat you alive!" He let her bridle go and tied one on the stallion, who caused no trouble.

On the way back through the grapevines he saw the Mormonhater outlined against his cook fire, holding onto his stick with one hand, gesturing with the other. Havek stood by, drinking coffee. Coming closer, South Boy saw he had a strange look on his face. It was blank, yet questioning, and there was a hint of awe in it.

As soon as the old man saw South Boy he began thumping the ground with his stick and shouted: "Get going! Get going! Mind what I say—*don't let the sun see him or anything of his!*"

Havek set his cup down on the ground and picked up his club. He said to South Boy: "I ride first, so I ride the mare. I won't need my bow, so you carry it!"

"Like hell I will!" cried South Boy. "Me, jugglin' two bows in the middle of trouble? Like hell I will!"

Havek picked up his bow, hung it across his body, stuck his arrows into the back of his belt, tied the end of the lead rope on the mare's jaw and, grabbing her by the mane, swung onto her back.

"And take it easy," South Boy called after him. "Her belly's sagging with water, and if you run her right away, you'll be catching your Piute afoot."

Havek didn't appear to heed him, but he let the mare take her own pace.

"Where in hell did I leave my grub bag?" South Boy demanded of no one in particular.

"Never mind your grub bag," the Mormonhater barked. "If this thing is done properly you will be back before noon. If it's not done, you'll not need any grub."

"But our trail goes north," said South Boy. "We won't be back here."

"You'll not go north of the witch's fire," said the Mormonhater earnestly. "I know that much. You'll come back here. Bring me my old rifle and the bullet bag, and by God—if you've done your job I'll give 'em to you."

"O.K., O.K.," said South Boy hastily, for there was frenzy in the old man's face.

He picked up his weapons with one hand, holding onto the lead rope with the other—for the little stallion was nickering and stomping, eager to follow the mare.

"Look into the bullet bag and be sure the Bible is there. It'll be wrapped in a blue cloth. But don't touch it! There'll be blood upon you. You can't touch it until you come back here and git purified."

"O.K.," said South Boy. The stallion spread, made water, and gave a shrill, blasting neigh. South Boy laid his hand on the horse's back and jumped. As they headed out on the mare's trail he heard the old man cry, "World's End!" He must have repeated it over and over because a long drawn-out "Wo-or-rld's E-end!" came to South Boy's ears some time later.

Havek had pulled up the mare and was waiting for him by the old stamp mill. "Does the old man know something, or is he just crazy?" he asked as soon as South Boy was alongside.

"He knows something, certainly. I don't know how much. I tried to find out for sure if he has the gift of farseeing, but he wouldn't tell me. What was he telling you?"

"One thing, and another," said Havek evasively. "A matter of foreign medicine. He says he has many medicines from many people."

"Well, he lived with the Piutes and the Navajos, and White Whiskers told me when he was young he lived with the Mexicans in Santa Fe and even went to school by the big church there. He lived with the Mormons once, and he lived here in this town in the old days with a Mojave woman, as he told us himself."

"If he learned other things as well as he learned Mojave, he must know a great deal," said Havek, and he slapped the mare.

They rode silently through a silent, steaming, ghastly world lit by a low, sickly moon with a ring around it. The trail they

followed was old, well worn, and rain-rutted. It had been made
by pack trains carrying down ore to the stamp mill a long time
ago. It had not been used lately. It was a ghost trail running
through a ghost country. Even the little greasewood bushes
seemed like shadows, with no substance at all.

"Maybe he knows something, and is a little crazy, too," was
Havek's final comment.

Up-river the northern horizon was still pulsating with re-
flected light. South Boy began listening for thunder, but heard
none. By and by he said: "Whether the old man knows anything or not is not important in this business. We have to kill
this crazy Piute, anyway."

Havek did not answer.

They came to the first big arroyo. The trail went down its
south bank like a running snake. Havek seemed to have lost
his urge for haste and let the mare pick her way cautiously.
South Boy looked past her and down to the arroyo bed, fifty
feet below. It was alive with flittering moon shadows, for gray-
white kangaroo rats and little jumping mice were dancing on
the sand. "Like something out of a fairybook," said South Boy,
half aloud. When they reached the sandy bed there was only
the lacework of a thousand little trails where the dancers had
been.

There Havek left the ore trail and rode towards the river,
then up-river along a sand bar that had been built at the foot
of the cliff since last high water. Under a scattering of loose
top sand the surface was hard. Havek broke the silence. "We
run now!" He raised his club high overhead and then brought
it forward in a sweeping arc as he heeled the mare into a lope.

Well, I hope he knows just where the Piute is, thought South
Boy. I sure wouldn't ride so brash if I was leading. But he said
nothing. He was beset by a numbing sense of unreality. All
this was happening to someone else. He was only a spectator.

They rode through young willows that were at times as high
as a man's head and as thick as the hairs on a dog's back, and at

times grew sparsely and not more than a foot high. Great piles of gray driftwood loomed up ahead and then vanished like the hulks of passing ships. The moon had sunk behind the cliff on the Nevada side of the river, and the night was deep in the canyon. They passed through a long stretch where the willows were very high and whipped South Boy's face. They passed through a patch where the willows had been cut to a stubble like the stubble in a grain field. Here the beavers had been working.

South Boy heard the first bat of the morning squeaking overhead, and he knew that the first light was not far away. A gust of wind, smelling hot and wet, came pushing down the canyon.

South Boy, thinking in Mojave, said to himself: "We have many things in our favor. We, being Amok Ave—people of the Three Mountains—riding in the shadow of the greatest of the three [Avequami was not in sight, but South Boy knew it was not far behind the Nevada cliff], riding by the place where Mustavilya made his house, through the canyon Mastamho made to wash away his father's ashes—we are on our own ground. The Piute is a trespasser here. And whatever is his cunning and whatever is his strength, he can't stand against a hawk-dreamer."

They came to a place where the ground between the river and the cliff was narrow and almost barren. Havek pulled up the mare and rode as close as possible to the wall of the cliff. Overhead, the sky was turning gray and the stars were fading. Havek held up his left hand to feel the wind. South Boy laid one arrow across his bow; the others, he gripped in his teeth. His heart went *thump-thump-thump*, slow and hard.

Ahead the cliff fell away to the right. The bar was wide and thickly grown with head-high willows. Close under the cliff was a procession of large trees. Havek's mare started off at an eager amble, skirting the trees.

The light was increasing. South Boy, watching ahead, saw

the first visible signs of the Piute—moccasin tracks around a torn-up rat's nest. The gust of wind increased, blowing over the little willows in great waves, such as the wind makes in a wheat field. All sound was lost in the moaning of the wind and the rush and tumble of the river.

Ahead was another great pile of driftwood extending more than halfway across the sand bar. Havek raised his club and motioned for South Boy to keep back. South Boy pulled up, and his horse began to dance, for the mare moved on.

The arrows he held in his teeth made his jaw ache.

Then he saw the Piute appear suddenly at the cliff end of the pile of driftwood. He was short, heavy, and barrel-chested. He wore only his high moccasins, a long filthy undershirt, and a little round, rimless cap that might have been the crown of an old derby. He was infinitely more primitive and animal-like than any man South Boy had ever seen. The old Springfield rifle was at his shoulder. Its barrel swiveled in a short arc from Havek to South Boy, back to Havek. His face was broad, flat, hollow-cheeked, with a broken nose and a mouth like a gash. It was battered and swollen, hideous with triple-distilled evil and all streaked with grease and wood ashes.

Havek's high, screaming squall rang out, above the river's noise. The mare leaped, and the club swung up. The Piute's rifle roared out, its thundering echoes rolling up and down along the wall of the canyon. Havek went flat on his pony's neck. His club swung low. The Piute's feet left the ground, the rifle flew out of his hands.

The mare made two jumps that carried her ten yards beyond the Piute, then she planted all four feet and Havek went sailing over her head to hit the sand like a sack of rags.

As South Boy remembered it afterwards, the fight on the sand bar had neither sense nor continuity. He let fly an arrow and raised the long wail, for he was certain Havek was dead. He jerked on the rope and threw his horse between the Piute and the rifle. But the Piute was gone—he had faded in the faint, treacherous light.

South Boy found himself crying, "Where—where?" when an arrow whistled by his ear. His pony, entirely out of control, cut around the drift pile. South Boy clung desperately with his knees, in spite of the fact that he knew he should be on the ground, for his six-foot Mojave bow was no horseman's weapon.

The Piute was running across a strip of beaver slashing, a short bow and short arrows in his hand, a big Mojave arrow sticking in his back. South Boy's pony was running after him. Havek had come to life and was yelling, "Head him off!" in English.

The Piute dived into the willows like a blackbird diving into a tule bed. Somehow South Boy managed to get an arrow across his bow and let drive at the spot where the crazy man had disappeared. He felt the willows whipping his face. After that all he could do was clamp his knees on the pony's barrel and ride. The little stallion was hunting the Piute on his own account, whether driven by hate engendered by past mistreatment, or by the same instinct that keeps a cutting horse on a cow's trail.

Out of nothing loomed a little pile of drift that was almost hidden by the thicket. The pony rose straight up. His neck slapped South Boy in the face. South Boy's mouth flew open. When he closed it he realized his arrows were gone.

It was in South Boy's mind to slide down and hunt arrows, but his horse still hunted the Piute, dodging around the drift and hurrying frantically through the whipping willows. As soon as he discovered he had lost his quarry he ran straight ahead and broke out onto the open sand bar.

The light was increasing rapidly. South Boy heard the Piute —then he saw him, about a hundred and fifty yards away, jumping up and down like an angry monkey, and shrieking,

not at South Boy, but at Havek, who from somewhere out
in the gray gloom, was shooting arrows at him.

The pony wheeled in his tracks and made for the Piute.

South Boy heard himself crying childishly, "Wait! I got to
get arrows!" But the pony bore down on the crazy man. There
was nothing South Boy could do but ride. He was quite close
when he realized that the Piute was out of arrows, too. The
Indian was facing him now, standing with his feet apart and
his knees sprung, ready to jump.

Then from out of the sky came a big, unpointed Mojave
hunting arrow and plunked into the sand right between the
Piute's feet. The Piute pounced on the arrow.

South Boy felt a pain in his left hand. He took his bow in
his right, and shook his left, and the arrow that was sticking
in the web of flesh between the thumb and the forefinger
flopped away. All this was in one pony-jump.

South Boy was crying like an angry child. He saw the Piute's
dirty distorted face with little crazy eyes, red-rimmed from
trachoma. The face disappeared. The Piute was running and
dodging. South Boy was beating him over the head and shoulders with his bow until it broke in his hand.

The next thing he knew the Piute jumped like a big, short-
legged frog. There was the river, and he was diving into it. And
South Boy himself was sailing over his pony's head.

The river closed over him. The water had a cold bite to it.
It felt good.

He wasn't more than a few seconds clambering out onto the
bank. He looked out over the river and saw nothing of the
Piute. Then an arrow popped up out of swirl in the red water,
turned slowly around and went floating downstream. It was
one of his own arrows. He recognized the Whisperer's skillful
fletching.

"Well, you're paid for," he said to the bleeding wound in his
left hand.

He started out at a trot down-river, looking over the water

for the Piute, while his right hand jerked at the front flap of his shirt. He ripped off a piece of it and began to bind his hand to stop the bleeding. He pulled the knot tight with his teeth.

The Piute broke water some distance out, rolled over on his back, filled his lungs, shrieked angrily at South Boy, and sank again.

South Boy yelled, "Havek, fetch that rifle!" His right hand was absently stuffing his shirttail back into his pants. Then it stopped.

"Well, damn me for a fool!" he said bitterly as his hand touched the gun he'd forgotten. He jerked it out, cocked it, and waited.

The Piute came up farther out and farther down the river and began swimming with a strong overhand stroke. It was a long shot, some sixty yards, but the light was better now. South Boy fired and saw the bullet kick the water some five feet downstream from the Piute's head. The Piute dived like a loon.

South Boy ran downstream and pulled the trigger again, directly the Piute reappeared. There was a dead click. The Piute kept on the surface of the water, breasting the current strongly, keeping his body pointed three-quarters upstream, so that the current would bear him across. South Boy sat down, rested his gun hand on his knee, and, carefully sighting three feet over the round cap that still clung to the Piute's head, he fired again and watched the bullet kick the water ten feet short and fifteen feet downstream.

"Shoots left," said South Boy. The range was out of all reason now but he held far upstream and far high, and fired, hoping for luck. But this time the bullet carried far to the right and high.

South Boy got to his feet, looked at the gun and cried out, in great heat, "Why, the dirty, lying, cheating sons-of-bitches!" For in his mind's eye was the glowing account of the gun's worth and accuracy as he had read it in the Chicago mail-order catalogue.

From up-river came the roar of the big rifle and there was a big spurt of water far beyond the Piute.

"I hope Havek held that rifle loose and broke his damn shoulder," said South Boy. "I told him to fetch it here!"

The Piute climbed slowly up the farther bank. He jerked an arrow out of his back and another out of his thigh and threw them into the river.

In one last spasm of anger, South Boy threw the worthless mail-order gun at a high arc over the river. It passed up and out of the cliff's shadow, and the first rays of the rising sun shone for a flickering instant on its nickel finish. It fell into the river some two hundred feet out. The Piute had already disappeared into the willows.

"Well, if this is what they call war, to hell with it," said South Boy. And he went wearily trudging up-river in search of Havek. "A crazy business!" he said to himself. "A worthless, crazy business, with everything going wrong."

Havek squatted on the bank a quarter of a mile upstream, rubbing his shoulder. He looked at South Boy and grinned. "That was smart, the way you kept the gun hid. I didn't know about it at all."

"Don't ever do business with those Chicago people," said South Boy, bitterly. "They're no-good liars. Why didn't you bring me that rifle?"

"I thought I could kill him myself, but the big gun jumps too much. Anyway, why worry about it? He'll die, maybe today, maybe tomorrow after the maggots start growing in his wounds."

Unlike South Boy, Havek seemed to be very well satisfied with the whole affair. He yawned widely and began stripping off his clothes. He was sweat-soaked, lazy, and happy, his face and clothes covered with dirt. He pulled the handkerchief from his head and dived into the river. Then he swam back and sat in the shallow water below the bank, washing the mud out of his hair.

He began singing softly to himself—his song growing louder as he started plastering his head with fresh mud, and finally becoming a great paean of triumph when he stood up and bound his head with the big handkerchief.

"What in hell is there to sing about?" muttered South Boy to himself.

He was still more disgusted when he saw that Havek had let the rifle drop into the sand. South Boy picked up the old Springfield, and with another piece of cloth from his depleted shirttail he began carefully removing the sand. The worst of it was, the protecting coat of skunk grease came off with the sand and he knew the rifle would rust quickly in the hot, muggy weather. It was his gun, too, as soon as he brought the Bible in the bullet bag back to the Mormonhater.

He looked around for the bullet bag. It, too, was lying in the sand where Havek had dropped it, a greasy old canvas coin bag with "$1000" still faintly discernible in black paint —probably discarded by some bank robber on the run from California and salvaged by the Mormonhater. The tie string was loose, but none of the contents had spilled out. South Boy picked it up and looked in. There was a square bundle carefully wrapped in blue cloth nestling among fifty or more greasy, finger-length cartridges of dingy brass with big blunt home-made bullets.

"That's the Bible, all right," said South Boy. He set the bag down, picked up the rifle and pulled some willow shoots through its bore, grumbling to himself because he lacked proper cleaning equipment.

Havek was still singing that part of "The Ravens" that concerns war. South Boy was wondering: Were the fights that were celebrated and described in the Great Tellings as glorious in the doing as in the telling—or were they senseless scrambles where men lost their heads and acted like angry children?

"A fine business," he said, looking at Havek.

But sarcasm was lost on the Mojave boy. "Yes. Surely. A

Great Thing was done. You saw it. I rode down a man with a rifle and hit him with a club. Like a striking hawk I rode, feeling no fear. Hawk Strikes. That's my name. You hear it."

"It's a wonder you didn't get shot," said South Boy, sourly.

"I did!" Havek turned his face and proudly displayed a raw bullet burn a half-inch wide just under his right cheek bone. "By so much I missed death"—and he measured half the tip of his little finger. "And you did a Great Thing! You rode him down and beat him with your bow. I saw it. Anyone can kill a dangerous man from a distance, but you struck him from close by and without fear. Take a name. Take a *good* name."

"I ain't any too proud of myself. The crazy man got away." South Boy was thinking that there would certainly be no glory in killing the sickening half-beast; but it was a job to be done, and he had bungled it.

"But he'll die!" Havek insisted. "And this way the death isn't directly on our hands. We got rid of him, still we don't have to smoke ourselves, which would be a hot job in this weather. Come, let's go home and sing about our new names. The old men will brag about us, surely."

He began eagerly pulling on his clothes, his eyes shining. South Boy knew he was thinking about how the old men of his clan, the best singers and the best orators, would lead him from one rancheria to another, crying his new name and glorifying his deeds. It was a ceremonial that rarely occurred these days, for few young men ever did anything worthy of it.

Suddenly South Boy said to himself: The trouble with me is, I'm thinking like a white man again. I should be proud like Havek and take a name. But, try as he would, he couldn't shake off the white-man thinking nor the feeling of defeat that it brought.

Maybe up in the Piute country— But he realized then that he would not be going to the Piute country.

He said, 'So we go south, now."

"Surely, surely," said Havek, picking up his bow.

"Then the Mormonhater is a farseer, all right. He said we'd go no farther north than the witch's fire."

"Yes, he certainly knows something."

At that Havek gave a short cry and clapped his hand over his mouth in a gesture of surprise, pointing across the river where the sun shone halfway down on the Nevada cliff, and said, "Hurry—we haven't done what must be done!" He hurried away into the willows.

South Boy stuffed the bullet bag into his shirt, picked up his rifle, and went trotting after Havek. For a moment he, too, had forgotten what the old man had said.

The first thing they found was the Piute's bow, a curious weapon half as long, twice as broad, and a third as thick as the Mojave bow. There was a layer of sinew strings glued to its back to keep it from breaking.

"It's a shame we have to burn it. It would be a good thing to show," said Havek, running this way and that, hunting arrows.

Then they came to the place where South Boy had chased the Piute and beat him with his bow. Havek let out a whoop and pointed down at the ground. There was a wavy line of dribbles marking the trail where the Piute ran.

"Scared-Piute-Makes-Water!" said Havek. "Take a name, South Boy. Take that name."

South Boy said: "No! That sounds all right to a Mojave. In English it's a dirty-joke name."

So they ran on. Havek began picking up arrows, some his own, some South Boy's—though they were all Havek's now because South Boy had broken his bow. Then Havek picked up a Piute arrow. It was short and iron-pointed, and its shaft was in two parts, spliced and bound with gut.

"A lot of silliness!" said Havek. "So much work to make an arrow."

They ran through the little willows and came out on the beaver-cut stubble beyond.

"Why don't you take a name?" asked Havek. "Take a good name. Like Hides-His-Gun or Piute Beater."

"Later. Later," answered South Boy, looking over his shoulder. The sunshine had reached the top of the willows on the Nevada shore. He said to himself: I don't understand this business about the sunshine, but we'd best do what the Mormon-hater said.

Together they ran across the stubble to the big driftwood pile and skirted the edge, going east toward the cliff. There, near the end of the tangle of logs, both boys froze like bird dogs. The little willows had been cut to make a clearing about six feet in diameter. In the middle of it was a small rock on which a small fire still smoldered. On one side of the rock was a little pile of prepared fuel. On the other side was a medicine pouch made from the whole skin of a small badger, apparently lying flat on the ground.

"Well, there's the witch's fire, like he told us," said South Boy, again pondering the business of farseeing. Maybe the old man had the gift. Maybe he just knew the ways of a Piute witch. He looked over his shoulder and saw the first rays of the sun striking the tips of the tallest trees on the Nevada shore and muttered, "Well, we found it in plenty time, anyway."

Havek stepped gingerly forward, dropped the Piute's bow and arrows across the rock, and spoke three sharp, jerky, Mojave phrases as he looked quickly away.

"Get wood! Cover everything! Burn quickly!"

"Uh-huh," said South Boy. "But I don't understand about that badger-skin bag. It looks empty."

He took three steps and picked up the bag. He gave a little grunt of surprise, for under it, laid close together and in an orderly pattern, waiting to be uncovered to the first rays of the new sun, was the witch's medicine: little bunches of owl feathers, little bunches of raven feathers, little bundles of dried hideousness that had been the entrails of animals and a contorted mummy that had been a fetus, animal or human.

Foreign filth, thought South Boy in disgust. The Mojaves had nothing like that.

Then it was he heard Havek's cry of horror. No death howl was more terrible, no ghost's cry more unexpected. He looked around to see Havek's knees buckle under him.

"Cover! Cover!" Havek gasped, and sat down very hard.

The badger skin dropped from South Boy's hand and fell across the objects of evil, hiding most of them.

"Sky-breaking! Sun-breaking! World's End!" shrieked Havek, his once stolid face wild with the fear of doom impending.

Genuinely alarmed, South Boy grabbed the little pile of fuel, put it across the rock and began blowing the fire furiously until it sprang into a blaze. He tore at the pile of drift, throwing every stick he could break loose into the fire. In two or three minutes he had covered the witch's gear, the altar rock and the entire area around it. The fire burned slowly, for although the wood was bone-dry, it was lifeless from having once been long in the water.

He looked back at the river. The sun had touched the water. Then he looked at Havek. Havek was leaning over, his arms wrapped around his middle, vomiting.

"For God's sake!" South Boy cried. "This is all foreign nonsense. You never heard any Mojave talk about the evil of owl feathers and such. It's nothing to us!"

Havek rolled up his eyes and gagged. The wind came downstream, and the fire suddenly took off with almost explosive force, the flames licked through the wood over the witch's gear, up the irregular face of the main drift pile, sending up great clouds of white smoke.

The sun had just reached the edge of the sand bar.

Chapter XI

DIES IRAE

Of the retreat from the place of the witch's fire, South Boy remembered very little. He knew he kept assuring himself: "This is foreign nonsense, this business of feathers and such. No Mojave, no white man either, would believe in such." Yet there was Havek, Mojave of the Mojaves, brave, dependable and able, and intelligent far beyond the ordinary, puking his guts out on the sand.

One thing, what evil there was it was burnt in good time. The whole near segment of drift pile was roaring in flames before the line of sunshine came creeping across the sand bar.

The heat was awful. Stupefied, uncertain, but driven by a kind of dogged stubbornness against whatever it was that had struck down Havek, South Boy ran back along the cliff to fetch the horses from where they were browsing along the mesquite and big willows. He kept saying to himself, "Now I am He-Who-Stands-Strong." He said this in Mojave and then added in English, "I'd better be, or we'll never get back to Hardyville."

He thought once he was defeated. The mare still hated him for the sting of the chloroform in that lion's scratch. She fought him, tooth and forefoot, every time he got near her. He could neither mount nor boost the helpless Havek onto her back. He collapsed in gasping, sobbing, sweat-drenched agony, when Havek suddenly got to his feet, cried, "Hardyville-old-man-doctor-make," threw himself on the mare's back, and rode her through the smoke-filled gap between the flames and cliff, babbling, "Foreign evil, doctor evil, World's End."

South Boy had just enough strength to grab his rifle and
hoist himself on the horse's back before the horse ran nickering after the mare.

When South Boy caught up with him, Havek was riding
with his chin on his chest, his body bent, and his shoulders
bowed. He still had his bow and arrows in his hand, but his
club was gone. He turned and pointed his bow at South Boy.
"Evil-uncovered!" Then pointed his bow at the sky. "World-
blasting!"

South Boy said, "Aw, shut up!" But the sky was appalling.
It was the color of a copper cent that had been scrubbed bright
with wet ashes. What was usually called a "copper sky" was
mild compared to it.

"World's End, or no World's End," he said in English,
"I'm getting this outfit back to Hardyville. The Mormonhater
must know something. He described the Piute's medicine fire
from afar."

Behind him he heard thunder for the first time, still far away
but loud enough to be heard over the talk of the river.

The wound in his hand began throbbing as he rode into a
sort of semi-oblivion that was like the worst of nightmares.
An endless time of pain and stress, and he rode out of it to find
he was among the ruins of Hardyville. Havek and the mare
were still ahead, but Havek lay across the mare's back like a
bedroll. South Boy's wet shirt was wrapped around the mare's
head and Havek's shirt was around the head of the stallion.
South Boy cudgeled his mind to remember how this happened, but nothing came of it.

The world was a hot rock, spewing steam. It was hardly
midmorning, but the horses walked like pack animals at the
end of a long day.

Directly South Boy saw the Mormonhater standing under
the big fig tree leaning on his stick.

The next thing he knew he was lying naked on the north
bank of the little ditch under the tree. There was salt meat in

his mouth. His sore hand was soaking in a Mojave pot full of hot water.

"For God's sake, haven't I boiled enough?" he said to a patch of copper sky that glared down at him through a space between the leaves.

"Keep that hand in there," said the Mormonhater. He was squatting over Havek, who lay like a dead man on the other bank of the ditch, smearing tar on the bullet burn on Havek's cheek while he sang a creaking unmusical song, intently, earnestly, anxiously. It was a doctor-singing—that much South Boy knew, though the words were foreign and the cadence strange.

"There's no sense to it," complained South Boy, looking at Havek. "One minute he was all right. The next minute he was sick, and then he was crazy." He felt all numb inside and empty, as if Havek had already died and left vacant a place where there had been a sense of comfort and companionship.

The Mormonhater made no answer until he had finished singing. Then he turned his haggard, sweat-streaked face toward South Boy and said: "The boy is witch-struck. You uncovered the witch medicine before you burnt it. That's bad. Some of it entered the boy. Some of it escaped to the sky. I am making four kinds of medicine to destroy it. I have made Piute medicine. I'll make Mojave medicine, Catholic medicine and Protestant medicine— Let me take a look at that hand."

He hopped across the ditch on his stick, took South Boy's hand out of the pot, and proceeded to dress it with pine tar and a white rag.

"Then will the world be blasted?" asked South Boy, half earnestly, half ironically.

The old man shook his head. "Not likely. The sun never saw the witch's medicine."

"But the witch got away!" said South Boy, indignantly.

"That's no great matter to us. His power was burnt with his medicine. When he recovers from his wounds he will become a mad coyote and kill a lot of people in Nevada before he dies, but with weapons, not witching."

South Boy closed his eyes. The river and the creaking water wheel made a background of sound overborne by the ripple of the ditch water, only six inches from his ear. His body, it seemed, was floating in a hot soup of many smells—of wet earth, mesquite smoke, and pungent arrowweed, of horse manure, fig leaves, and his own sweat. He was floating between worlds without purpose or destination. The road he had chosen had closed before him at the place of the witch's fire. Havek was gone. There was no one to lead him. He kept saying to himself, "Where do I go? Where do I go?"

He heard the Mormonhater begin singing the Latin hymn "Dies Irae." His eyes opened. He asked sharply, "What's that?" and the Mormonhater said: "The Day of Wrath. It's part of the medicine I learned in Santa Fe." And he went on singing. So South Boy said to himself, I'll remember this day by that singing, forever.

He stewed in the soup of smells and dozed, thinking: It's the Mormonhater who should take a new name this day. We will give him a big feed and call him "Many Medicines." He has the soul of several men.

He had heard of very great doctors who were so possessed. Maybe that's why he acts so cohiva-michiva. Maybe it's because he has so many kinds of knowledge.

He felt ashamed for last night's quarrel; and with a new respect for the old man he began to feel better, and he went to sleep.

When he awoke a short time later his respect was increased, for the Mormonhater was chanting a part of the long "Goose" singing, exactly like a Mojave doctor—the same kind of voice and the same manner of singing. Like last night when he told us the story of the sand-hill fight—he is an old Mojave.

So South Boy again slept.

The next time he awoke, the Mormonhater was reading

from the Bible—sitting cross-legged, his back against the trunk of the tree, with the protecting blue cloth in which the Bible had been wrapped lying on his knee. His voice was the voice of a back-country preacher reading from his pulpit.

South Boy looked across the ditch and saw Havek lying on his belly sleeping like a child.

Many Medicines has cured him, surely. I'll stay here with the old man and learn his many medicines. If anyone comes to take me away, I'll hide in the brush. By the time the old man dies, I'll know everything. I'll be a great man, all by myself, forever.

He thought he had found a new road and destination, and so with his mind at ease he went to sleep again. When he woke up next it was with a feeling of great relief. He felt good, but rather dazed. He rolled over on his back and looked up at the patch of sky between the fig leaves. There was no glare of burnished copper. The patch of sky was covered by slate-gray clouds coming from the south. There on the ground was a hot, wet breeze coming from the north. South Boy lay still for a moment, dreaming that he was up in a balloon carried along by the strong cool wind that was pushing those clouds. Once when he was younger he had been able to dream like that for hours, but lately such dreams came only in flashes.

The Mormonhater was sitting farther down on the ditch bank, rewrapping the knife wound on his leg. "Nice clean cut," he said, seeing South Boy was awake. South Boy thought, "He's different again. This time he is himself, the-man-of-the-river. Maybe he'll talk about Tom Paine."

"Never had a nicer cut in all my life," said the Mormonhater. He stood up and tested his strength on his leg. Evidently he decided against walking on it unassisted, for he leaned over and picked up his stick.

It was a little disconcerting to South Boy to have to make the usual white man's talk when he himself was thinking like an Indian; so he tried to conjure the Mormonhater back into another mood by speaking to him in very polite Mojave, such as a respectful young man would use to an old man of great wisdom. He said: "Havek sleeps well. Four medicines cured him, surely."

"Yes, my doctoring is very good—he'll wake up as fresh as a daisy," said the Mormonhater, half in Mojave, half in English.

"The witch got away, three-wounds-carrying, river-swimming. Will he join the war up-river?"

"Oh, that!" said the Mormonhater in disgust. "That's no war. Some poor, cheated, half-starved Piutes killed some sheep, got caught at it, and killed a sheepherder. Now they're all dead or in jail or hiding out in the desert from the sheriff's posse. I intended to tell you last night that chasing up there to find a war was just foolishness. Them days is over, son."

"War is nothing much, anyway," said South Boy. "But this matter of farseeing and other knowledge. That's a good thing. I would travel with you and learn all that. I could help you trap and hunt and gather honey. My help would be a good thing for you, and your knowledge would be a good thing for me."

The Mormonhater looked at him sharply and said, "No!"

"Why?" South Boy demanded.

"Because I'm the last of my kind. There ain't going to be any more like me. My day is done. My times is gone. These is the times of steam trains and irrigating ditches. You go find somebody to teach you about steam trains and irrigating ditches. You got no business in a mud boat with me." The Mormonhater hobbled to the house. He came back in a moment with the Springfield, the bullet bag and South Boy's traveler's rations.

"Here's your gear. I put a bullet mold in the bag with the cartridges. When this boy wakes up, you-all better get going. They'll be a big rain, by and by."

South Boy pushed himself slowly to his feet. "Does learning

about steam trains and irrigating ditches mean I got to go
away to some white school?"

"Well, you can't learn things like that running around
through the mesquite. They're part of civilization, and you
got to go to a civilized place to learn about them."

"To hell with them!" said South Boy. He leaned over the
ditch and began washing his face to hide his tears.

He washed himself all over finally, and climbed into his
clothes and sat down with his ration bag between his knees,
nervously chewing sweet screw beans without appetite and
staring at the old man, who sat with his back against the fig
tree, his stick in his hand and his chin sunk down on his chest.

Hah! Cohiva-michiva, South Boy accused, silently. Gratefully he remembered the matter of Nebethee. Well, old Four
Medicines might know something, but his great-ape theory
was certainly crazy. If Nebethee was a gorilla, why hadn't
anybody ever seen his tracks? And gorillas, being animals,
had to breed and die. Where was the she-ape, and where were
the pups? Who had seen them?

Then he heard a moan from Havek. He was waking up.
His blinking eyes were staring at nothing. His face was a
mask of stupidity.

South Boy glanced over at the Mormonhater and saw he
was looking at Havek with surprise and concern.

"He's still witched," said the old man. "You had no business
lifting that badger skin. You let too much evil fly up."

"Look, why wasn't *I* witched? *I* lifted the skin. *I* was the
closest to the witch medicine. *I* looked right at it, and *I* wasn't
witched."

"That's because you was ignorant," said the Mormonhater.
"I told this boy about the awful power of owl feathers and
raven feathers and the other medicine, and told him what would
happen if he looked at them."

South Boy gave a crow of triumph. "So that's it! Havek
isn't witched. He's just scared on account of what you told

him!" He got up, tied his ration bag, and slipped the loop of string over his shoulder. He put the bullet bag inside his shirt and picked up his rifle. "Come on, Havek. You ain't hurt. Let's travel."

Out of South Boy's mind came the question, Travel where? and he turned his back so that no one could see the trouble in his face.

Havek, finding himself naked, made babbling cries until he found his clothes, then dressed himself clumsily. He saw his bow and arrows, picked them up, and went stumping off through the grapevines toward the hayfield where the horses grazed listlessly. The Mormonhater had loosened the ropes from their jaws and tied them around their necks. Havek caught the mare's rope and mounted like a fat squaw. The mare whirled around and headed for the house; the stallion came whimpering after her.

"He's not bad now," said the Mormonhater. "I got most of the witchin' out of him. The rest will wear off by night. You better follow him, though, and see he don't hurt himself."

"Let me have a canteen," said South Boy. "I don't know where he'll lead me."

Chapter XII

DEATH AND THE DOCTOR

Havek led straight down the old trail to Fort Mojave. He rode badly, without regard for his mount, sometimes flogging her with his bow in an attempt to make her run, sometimes letting her lag or even turn around and start drifting north.

South Boy read all this from his trail, but the mare was out of sight before he got the canteen filled. He rode at a steady running walk, holding back the eager little stallion who didn't seem to mind the heat in his anxiety to find the mare. South Boy himself was swimming in sweat before he had gone five hundred yards, canteen strap over one shoulder, grub-bag string over the other, cartridge bag bulging his shirt front, and the heavy rifle across his legs. No matter the burden, he felt an insistent urge to keep all his property right with him.

He kept saying to himself: "I wish I had a saddle. You can tie things to a saddle."

Affliction had the opposite effect on Havek. He left Hardyville with only his bow and arrows, and before he had gone a mile he began dropping or throwing away arrows and he had only his bow when South Boy's horse found his mare at the rancheria where the two boys had played raid-the-enemy two days ago.

The mare stood in the middle of the barren ground between the winter house and the ramada, her head hanging, her legs spread. Havek, his head going around like a Johnny-owl's, was staring in bewilderment, crying, "Gone! Gone!"

The rancheria was deserted.

South Boy rode up alongside, unscrewed the cover of the canteen and handed it to Havek. "They're just gone some place," he said. Havek looked at South Boy as though he were a stranger, but he took the canteen and drank. When he made a move to throw it away South Boy grabbed it. Havek's heels struck the mare's ribs. "Where are my people?" he said. "Where are my people?" And he rode away, blindly seeking his kin.

After a mile or so South Boy said, "Look, you are a Hawk-dreamer. It's not fitten you act this way."

Havek pointed to the sky and said: "World's End! World's End! The clouds move against the wind."

"You make me sick," said South Boy. "The wind's different up there. I've seen it that way before, and you have, too."

Havek stared at him, blank-faced, the sweat standing out on his forehead in great greasy drops that did not seem to run down as sweat properly should. Then he muttered: "Old-man-of-my-people I must find. Or maybe I die—or maybe I'm dead now. I don't know." He wiped his face with his sleeve, then hit the mare with his bow. She moved off down-river, un-steadily.

South Boy said, bitterly, "If she founders I suppose it will be me that'll be walking." He added, "If I can get you to Yellow Road's camp you'll be all right. He'll know what to do with you."

Some time later both horses turned off the trail of their own accord, and before South Boy could do anything to stop them they trotted down a wild-horse trail and into Snake lagoon, where they stood belly-deep and buried their heads in the brackish, soup-warm water. They didn't drink much because they had already drunk their fill of sweet river water that day.

South Boy said, "That's lucky, or we'd both be walking."

"Maybe I die," said Havek. "I feel the foreign-devil eating my belly."

That's worse than World's End, thought South Boy. That's a Mojave idea. So he slapped the mare on the rump and said: "Come on. Let's go see Yellow Road."

They were no more than a mile or two from Yellow Road's camp, and South Boy thought surely he was finished with strange and unaccountable happenings for that day. Yet right there in front of him he saw a tall man wearing a shirt and no pants with a bundle of wet fish nets dangling over one shoulder. The man was running. In that stupefying heat he was running at the shambling, distance-consuming gait of a River Indian. Not another living thing had they seen since they left Hardyville.

A moment later he heard the man singing. South Boy couldn't understand the words, but he recognized the rhythm as the "Goose" singing dreamed by "doctors." Then he saw that the big man was real enough. He was Down-River-Old-Man, a doctor of great repute.

Havek began slapping his mare. He was first to draw up alongside the doctor, but when he opened his mouth to speak no sound came out. He only gasped and rolled his eyes like a spent runner. So South Boy spoke up.

"What is the power of owl feathers and raven feathers?"

"Uh! To make talk for old women," said Down-River-Old-Man.

South Boy looked at Havek, and Havek brought his hand to his mouth in a gesture of embarrassment.

"They were from a witch's pouch," added South Boy. "Surely a great foreign-evil, making World's End."

"A great foreign nonsense," said the doctor.

"What does it mean when the clouds move so?" asked Havek, pointing up.

"Rain like hell purty quick," the doctor grunted—in English, to show his disdain.

Havek's face suddenly relaxed and sank into heavy, sullen lines.

Well, thought South Boy, that's the end of witchin' for now. He immediately felt relieved. He knew that Havek would be sullen and silent for a long time, but he would be entirely out of danger.

Then Down-River-Old-Man looked sharply at Havek. "You, boy, are one of Yellow Road's kin. Why aren't you up at his camp? The call went out yesterday. Where were you?"

Havek looked down at the ground and said: "Far. Far. We've been up the river, traveling—name-traveling—"

"Name-traveling? Name-traveling on horseback!" croaked the old man in a fury. All this time he was shambling along at such a rapid pace that the boys had to thump their ponies into a trot every now and then. Still he kept just a little ahead, and he spoke with his head turned and his chin resting on the wet fish net. "Are you a cripple? Are you a woman? Are you a Mexican? Are you a Real Person at all? Why, when I went name-traveling I ran naked for four days and nights until I came to the Tehachapi Mountains, and there I slept in deep snow. Then I ran four days more and saw the Great Sea. I saw a thousand places, and I knew them all by name. I saw a thousand towns, and I heard ten different languages. All that time I never left off running. Horses! Why, horses got in my way. 'Get off my trail,' I yelled, and kicked them aside."

Havek could not stand this sort of rebuke. He slid off the mare and went trotting after the old man. The mare stopped where he left her, her head hanging. South Boy let her be.

Havek called to the doctor: "What's my kin gathered for? Is my uncle dying? What part have you had in that?"

South Boy fought his horse past the mare, marveling at the way Havek was recovering.

"Blame your lazy, horse-riding relatives if Yellow Road dies," shouted the doctor. "They should have sent for me yesterday. Not till this morning comes a fat slouch of a horse-rider. I was fishing. I told him he was too late, but I'd do what I could. I began singing right away, for I knew at once that a spider was spinning her trails around Yellow Road's heart.

Being a farseer, I could see even from there that she had made two trails already and was spinning the third. So I began singing. Yesterday I could have stopped the spider, surely. Today, I don't know. If she makes three roads, it's bad. If she finishes the fourth before I can stop her, the old man is dead. Shut up, and let me sing."

He turned his head and began singing "The Goose" again.

Havek was crying; great tears streamed down over the tar-smeared bullet burn across his face. South Boy saw them as he rode up alongside.

They were now in sight of the camp perched on the mesa's rim. The wailing of the assembled kinsmen came plainly through the thick air. It was a sad thing to hear, but in spite of that it was wholesome, and normal, and sane—it made South Boy feel he was on solid earth for the first time that day. Suddenly he was hungry. He untied the string on his ration bag and began munching screw beans.

At the foot of the mesa they encountered tangible evidence that Yellow Road had already signified that he expected to die. A big black dog lay dead, his mouth gaping. He had gone to scout the trail that Yellow Road's soul would follow to the cold, misty, topsy-turvy land of shadows.

If by mischance the dog had been killed after the man's death, the dog would have annoyed him the whole journey, yapping and snapping at his heels.

A little farther on lay a horse with its throat cut. It was not so often that a horse was killed at a man's death. South Boy concluded this must have been the animal ridden by the messenger who had gone for the doctor. It had probably foundered, and therefore had been cheap sacrifice.

Up the switchback trail strode the tall, untiring old doctor. South Boy thought, There's one man almost as good as he brags. Behind the doctor trotted Havek, his head down, weeping. The little stallion bearing South Boy and his mass of equipment came toiling along a considerable distance behind.

As soon as the doctor's head appeared above the rim of the mesa, the wailing abruptly tapered off and died into a sullen silence that was broken by two sharp outbursts of hysterical accusations from two different women. Men's voices came in an angry, rumbling undertone. Then Havek appeared. A number of women set up a peculiar mourning cry, "Lil-lil-lil." South Boy could hear the patter of their feet as they ran to meet the boy and surround him. They would be the old women—some of them relatives, some professional mourners—who surrounded each of the younger relatives at every cremation and made sure they cry properly.

When South Boy reached the top of the mesa he saw Havek kneeling about a hundred feet this side of the ramada, surrounded by a circle of squatting old women—each a bundle of dingy calico, each one urging him to wail and weep, for the great man, the old man, the great hota, the great war captain, would be gone, gone, gone!

As for the doctor, he stalked over to the far side of the ramada, took one look at Yellow Road, who now lay on some new cotton blankets, shook his head, and walked over to one of the supporting posts, leaned nonchalantly against it, standing on one leg, with the other knee raised, the other foot braced against the post, making a figure four. He glanced boldly around, folded his arms, and spat defiantly.

"Too late, too late," he said. "Yesterday you quarreled and argued. Some said, 'We'll call in this doctor.' Others said, 'We'll call in that doctor.' Some said, 'Call in nobody.' So you wasted a day while the spider went on spinning. Now she's making the fourth road. It's too late."

A tall middle-aged woman in a green silk dress trimmed with yellow bands—one of Yellow Road's daughters—cried out, "Your mother, your father, your father's father, all dead!"

"Surely," said the doctor. "They weren't foolish enough to live too long. Yellow Road has lived too long. Ask him. He will tell you he's unlucky. A brave man does not wish to live too long, nor does a doctor. I do not wish to live too long. I stand here. Is there a man of your kin who wants to step over here and kill me?"

All this South Boy heard and saw as he rode between the ramada and the mesa edge. He saw there was no one under the bird's-nest granary; so he was going there to divest himself of his burdens and rest awhile. He was very tired, and he could feel the horse trembling under him.

He slipped off with a weary grunt and dropped rifle, grub bag, canteen and then pulled the bullet bag out of his shirt, for the loading tool inside of it had been prodding his belly. "Gimme a saddle after this," he said.

Hardly was he on the ground when the horse, that had seemed so spent, threw up his head, whirled around, and bugled shrilly. He went trotting back to the trail and promptly disappeared over the rim to find the mare.

South Boy had a sinking, sickly feeling of utter loneliness as he sat down among his possessions and unscrewed the cover from the canteen. Havek had found his kin and the end of his affliction. The horse would find the mare down in the mesquite. South Boy took a sip of tepid water, and it tasted bitter. He had found nothing. He was all alone on a trail that led nowhere.

His sense of loneliness was emphasized by the fact that no one paid the least attention to him. If he had been a relative, he would have been met by the wailing women. If he had been a stranger, he would at least have been stared at—with curiosity, if not hostility. But he was South Boy, neither kin nor stranger, a vacuum between two worlds.

Under the ramada the doctor leaned against the post and glared around him. No one seemed to be immediately anxious to accept his offer. Two or three middle-aged men looked angry enough and spoke indignantly among themselves, but none of them made an overt move. The woman in the green dress did come closer and kept up her vindictive name-calling. The rest of the thirty or forty people under the willow-roof went back to mourning, each little group wailing its grief in one of several traditional ways.

On either side of Yellow Road sat his two wives, their heads bent, their hair over their faces. They moaned, their thick bodies rocking slightly to and fro. At Yellow Road's head stood one of his cousins, a short-haired man, a hota, a great singer, and a man of consequence who had a good job in the railroad yards at Needles. He sang "The Nichiva" which was the singing that Yellow Road had dreamed, and not his own. This he would sing as long as Yellow Road lived. There were two different groups, men and women, weeping around the old men who were "funeral preaching," telling the story of the creation of the Mojave world and the origin of the Mojave customs in the characteristically sharp, jerky phrases. Other groups, standing or sitting, wailed or wept. Everybody was sweating prodigiously, and although this brought them little relief in the steaming, windless atmosphere no one seemed to notice the heat.

Outside the ramada were circles of wailing women, each surrounding one or more of Yellow Road's younger relatives, most of whom were of school age and wore school uniforms.

"Ho! He was brave! Ho! He led the fighting! The Piutes feared him, and the foreign Apaches sang about him. Now he'll be ashes. Gone forever . . ." So cried the wailing women.

Tears began running down South Boy's cheeks as he sat munching screw beans out of his sack.

One of the women moved a little to one side, and he saw Yellow Road's face as he lay very still on his blanket. It was haggard and emaciated beyond description, but it was calm—the only face there that was devoid of emotion.

A tall, long-haired man wearing a loincloth and a long white undershirt, new and clean, appeared over the mesa's rim. He carried a long staff and a bundle wrapped in red and white calico which he dropped on the large pile of combustible goods—cloth, weapons, and various wooden articles—collected at the far corner of the ramada. These articles had been contributed by the relatives to be burnt at the cremation.

South Boy gathered his own possessions a little closer to him, vexed and disturbed by the thought of this senseless destruction of property. That the dead man's own property should be destroyed, he could understand. The Mojaves could tolerate no reminder of the dead, and that which belonged to a man was in a way part of him and must be obliterated at his death or become an offense to the living.

But this business of the relatives of a dead person burning their own perfectly good and sometimes brand-new property at the cremation—this irked South Boy beyond words. A silly, senseless, show-off business, he told himself. They just do it to show the neighbors they have the stuff to burn.

Yet at the back of his mind he knew there was more to it than that. There was the instinct the people had to divest themselves of their possessions in time of stress, to throw away everything—just as Havek had thrown away his arrows. *Chuplic*, "throw-away," that was what they called the goods piled up over there to be burned at the cremation.

South Boy, being white, gathered his possessions to him in time of stress, as a setting hen gathers her eggs.

Meanwhile, the man in the white undershirt shot an angry look at the doctor and went under the ramada to join the group still discussing the doctor's challenge.

White Undershirt had a hooked nose and an angry face. A few words from the others, and he began pounding the earth with the butt of his stick.

The woman in the green dress joined the group. She spoke passionately, in a high keening voice. The tall staff pounded the ground with greater vigor. The doctor, who was close enough to hear everything that was said, did not move. He leaned against his post, fish net still draped over his shoulder, his arms folded, haughty, defiant—entirely indifferent to his fate.

White Undershirt stalked towards him, his staff smiting the

ground with each deliberate step. The woman in the green dress walked at his left side, the other men coming a pace or two behind. The singer kept singing, and the preachers kept on preaching; but several of the mourners stopped their wailing to watch.

White Undershirt stepped in front of the doctor and demanded in a high voice that he begin singing at once, and sing properly, for if Yellow Road should die his death would be on the doctor's head.

The doctor looked disgusted.

South Boy thought, Why should he sing over a man everybody counts as dead already? It made him angry to think that people like Yellow Road's kin, whom everybody considered more intelligent than the average, should take such an unfair attitude in the matter. He knew he was angry because he was thinking like a white man, but he didn't reprove himself for it.

White Undershirt gave a cry and raised his staff.

There came a shout of warning from one of the rear guard. The staff was lowered before it struck.

Over the rim of the mesa appeared a low-crowned, stiff-brimmed California Stetson. Under it was a thick-bodied Indian in a sweat-darkened blue shirt. He had a gun belted about his middle. He was sitting in a big, well worn stock saddle on a bay horse.

As the horse stalked slowly across the mesa the protesters quietly turned their backs on the doctor and drifted away among the mourners.

The doctor gave absolutely no sign of relief—neither by change of facial expression nor by movement of body.

The man on horseback, but for his short hair and dress, was typical Mojave, but he carried himself with the bored, half-truculent air that marks the policeman everywhere. The sight of him gave South Boy almost as much of a jolt as it had given the man in the white undershirt. He was thinking: Either my father or my mother came home and has started looking for me. Word must have been sent to the Fort, and this policeman was sent to fetch me! I guess that means I'll be sent away to school pronto.

He sat still and chewed on the beans. There being nothing else to do, he tried to adopt the stoical, scornful attitude of the doctor. The policeman swung out of the saddle and stopped under the ramada. He glanced at Yellow Road, turned, and came slowly toward the granary, walking with the stiff-legged gait of a horseman rather than the loose-jointed, easy shamble of a River Indian.

South Boy began reasoning with himself: My mother certainly wouldn't come home in this heat. If my father came home he'd be too busy to miss me; or, if he did, he'd think I was visiting.

The policeman glanced back over his shoulder at the ramada. Then he looked at South Boy, nodded, and slumped to the ground, stretching his legs out in front of him.

South Boy said, "Hi yuh, Joe," as a white man speaks to a white man.

The policeman took off his hat, wiped his forehead with his sleeve, and said: "Christ, it's hot! Gimme that canteen, will yuh?"

South Boy handed it over. His heart lifted, in spite of lingering foreboding as to the man's purpose.

The policeman gulped noisily and handed the canteen back. "If this heat keeps up there's going to be a lot more people dying, and they won't be Mojaves, either. Sure hope it rains." He looked speculatively up at the hurrying clouds.

"Well, it's the fourth day," said South Boy. "It might rain."

Both nodded wisely.

By and by the policeman said, "The agency doctor's sick, so they sent me to see they don't burn the old man too soon."

So that was it. The policeman had been sent from the Fort to prevent a premature cremation—an event too frequent in the past because of the hysterical haste of the mourners in obliterating their dead. South Boy thought of "Danny the Dancer," who for a short-bit would gyrate on a withered leg to amuse the saloon crowd down in Needles. Danny's leg had been burnt to the bone in a cremation fire.

"But Yellow Road's plenty old. When he's dead, he'll stay dead."

"Yeh, but I'm going to make sure," said the policeman.

"Yeh, you gotta make sure," echoed South Boy. Now he was terrifically glad the policeman was there. He was practical, solid, and understandable in a world that had become confusing, unstable, and illogical. He was somebody you could talk to. South Boy opened his ration bag and handed it over. The policeman took a handful of screw beans and began chewing vigorously.

"Looks like we might be having some doctor trouble here."

South Boy nodded. "Why don't he show some sense and clear out?"

"Just stubborn," said the policeman. "Like a lot of old men." Then he added, "More people are coming."

People were arriving in little groups both up the trail and over the mesa. They were not of Yellow Road's clan. They gathered some distance from the ramada, and as yet only the old women joined in the wailing, though occasionally an old man would take to "preaching."

"Don't see that woman, yet," said the policeman.

"Which'n?"

"She was yonder"—the policeman pointed down towards the flat with his chin, the only typical Indian gesture he had yet made—"sitting under a mesquite tree having a baby; but she said she was all right, so I come on. I told her she shouldn't be running around on a hot day so close to her time, but she told me she wasn't going to miss the 'cry' on account of a baby. I suppose I'll have to go back down and see what's the matter. Hate to have two things on my mind like this."

"Uh-huh," agreed South Boy with considerable feeling. "I know just how it is. If I ain't had two things on my mind the last three days, it's been six. Couple of times it just about throwed me."

The policeman looked at him with interest. "You sound like you had growed up all of a sudden."

South Boy said: "Well, something's happened to me. I thought maybe it was just Crazy Weather."

The policeman's mind had drifted back to his own pressing problems of birth and death. "If she's in trouble I'll have to round up some old woman to help her, and I'll have a hell of a time."

"Uh-huh," said South Boy. He looked over the crowd. Every old woman was enjoying herself at the top of her voice.

"You could take my horse and herd a couple for me, if we have to—"

"Huh-uh," said South Boy in decisive negation. "That'd be worse than herding weanlings."

"Well, do you know how to take a mirror and test a body for the breath of life?"

"Uh—I've been told, but I've never done it."

"Never mind. Here she comes!" And they both leaned back in obvious relief.

A stolid heavy woman of early middle age appeared over the rim of the mesa. Her movements were easy and leisurely, except for those of her lower jaw. She was vigorously chewing gum. She sat down on a little rise of ground beyond the ramada, bared a fat breast and to it she held the newborn child, wrapped in her tahoma. Even at that distance South Boy could see the expression of peace and complacency on her broad busy face. It put him somewhat in mind of a ruminating cow. She looked at everyone but spoke to no one, after the usual manner of an Indian at any public place.

Every now and then she would look down at her baby and smile. As she had ceased to be a public responsibility, the policeman and South Boy paid no more attention to her.

Suddenly South Boy asked, "Say, did you hear any more about the trouble up north?"

"Sure," said the policeman. "The superintendent got word by telephone yesterday. The damn fools is all jailed."

South Boy thought, The Mormonhater was farseeing in that matter, too.

"Sa-ay!" said the policeman. "There was supposed to be a couple of bronco Piutes at the top of the valley day before yesterday. Somebody raised a long yell, and me and two other fellers went up there, but we didn't cut no sure sign—"

"One Piute," South Boy broke in.

"Huh?"

"Just one. He was bad crazy. He knifed the Mormonhater up to Hardyville and stole a rifle. *This rifle*." South Boy picked up the old Springfield and laid it across his knees, slapping the butt a couple of times for dramatic emphasis. "Well, me and Havek happened along, and the old man told me if we could get the rifle back he'd give it to me. He done bought himself a Winchester a while back."

"Sure, I know," affirmed the policeman. "Did you get the crazy man?"

"Well, we got the rifle. We jumped the Piute up in the canyon, and he shot Havek. Look over there—when he raises his head, you can see the bullet burn on his face. Well, Havek knocked the gun out of his hand; but the crazy man got away, and we had a fight on our hands. All through them little willows—like fighting a flea on a dog's back. But we hit him with three arrows, and he jumped into the river.

"Of course we got self-defense all right," South Boy added hastily, having been well schooled by the Foreman in how to present his story to the Law in such a case. "He shot first."

"Sure. Sure. But you ain't let the crazy man get away!"

"Well, he swam the river all right, but he had three arrows in him."

"Why in hell didn't you use that rifle?"

"How in hell could I? He was all over the sand bar, and me after him—Havek brought the gun and took one shot at him, but you know he ain't hardly ever shot a rifle—"

"But if a crazy man's loose I gotta go up there," wailed the policeman. "That's a hell of a trip in this weather."

As if I don't know! thought South Boy. Aloud he said, "Three arrows, and Havek hit him with a club, and I bust my bow over his head—"

The policeman went into a deep study. Then he said: "All right, I'll report him dead. You and the Mormonhater can back me up if there's any doubt about it. I sure don't want to have to chase up there and cross the river and everything just to find a dead loco—anyhow that's off the reservation and out of my jurisdiction."

"Hey, your report," said South Boy nervously. "Will Havek and me have to testify to something?"

"Heck, you'll be heroes! My God, don't you remember the trouble that last loco made for us? If you killed this one, you should get a medal."

"Yeh, but the only thing is that the Mormonhater said this Piute's a witch, and if he makes that kind of talk before the superintendent, the superintendent will say this here is another case of witch killing, and then he won't believe anything we say about anything, because I know he comes from Zuñi where there's been plenty of witch killings and he's sure dead against it."

The policeman was silent for a moment, and then he said: "Forget it. I won't make any report, and there won't be any investigations. It all happened off the reservation, anyhow. So what the hell?"

So a sense of comradeship and understanding between South Boy and the policeman grew.

"You know, Joe," said South Boy, "it sure does me good to talk to you. You're smart. You can figure things out white way and Indian way both, and by golly, you don't get caught in the middle, either!"

The policeman looked pleased. "You're plenty smart yourself, South Boy. I mean, you keep books and everything, or so they tell me—"

"Yeh, but I ain't smart about figgering things out like you, Joe." South Boy looked at him earnestly. "I can think like an Indian sometimes, then I can think like a white man. But like now—I get caught in between—I don't know how to bring them two kinds of thinking together. I just get to fighting my hat, and I can't figger nothing—"

The policeman looked puzzled. "Well—I don't know how to help you out. They had my head spinning for a while, but things get straightened around. You know, they sent me away to the big school in Phoenix, and then clear back to Haskell—"

"They want to send me away to school, and it just scares hell out of me."

The policeman laughed. "You'll get over it. I was scared, too."

"But, Joe, you was sent to an Indian school. If I could go to an Indian school, I'd be all right— It's the idea of being shut up with a lot of strange white people."

"Say," said the policeman. "If you don't think some of the Indians I ran into back East weren't strange enough! Why, they weren't any more like Mojaves than anything. White people aren't half so foreign. Hey, look! The old man must be about gone. Here comes the first of the logs!"

Over the rim of the mesa came four toiling men, each pulling on a lariat that was tied to a huge cottonwood log. They were big, long-haired men in shirts and loincloths. They sang as they came, digging their hard bare feet into the gravel as they dragged the log through the spectators to a spot on the mesa out to the east of the ramada where other men were digging a fire hole seven feet by four.

Next came a mesquite log borne on the shoulders of one

man who stood up straight under its weight. His lips moved, but the song could not be heard over the noise. It was the Whisperer.

South Boy tried to go on with his talk with the policeman, but the air of approaching climax that hung over the assembly was too distracting. The policeman got up and looked over at Yellow Road. The bay horse came over and nuzzled him. Absently he slipped its bridle, reached into the granary, filled his hat with mesquite beans, and dumped them on the ground a few feet away. He said: "You might as well eat them. The rest will be burnt up in a minute."

South Boy was saying, "I wish I could figger out—" when a sudden pandemonium broke loose under the willow-roof. A cry of anguish that made the previous wailing seem like silence arose from around the dying man and spread outward to the outermost periphery of the crowd. It was caught up by the log bearers coming up the trail and the late-comers straggling over the mesa. And above the general cry came the high cry of the loon from those who had dreamed the loon-dreaming.

The policeman put on his hat, pushed it to the back of his head, adjusted his gun-belt, and said: "Come on, kid. Let's go. I want you for a witness, in case there's any argument."

South Boy's own problem had been submerged by this climax in this drama of death. He picked up his rifle, a visible token of his quasi-official capacity, and stalked after the policeman, unconsciously imitating his stiff-legged walk and bored manner.

A while back he had wished the rifle was a carbine, less awkward to manage on a horse, and less heavy. Now he was glad the barrel was long to lend him dignity for the occasion. The crowd gave way a little, although there was no pause in the wailing, neither did anyone appear to see either of them.

When they came to the place where Yellow Road lay, the policeman took a hand mirror out of the pocket of his shirt and, bending down, placed it over Yellow Road's nose and mouth. South Boy ground the butt of his rifle and leaned on the long barrel, elbow over the muzzle, waiting.

"I don't know whether this works when it's so hot," grumbled the policeman.

The wailing died. One of Yellow Road's women began whimpering like a puppy, protesting this obscene delay in properly disposing of the body. She was still seated. She seized the barrel of South Boy's rifle above the lock and pulled herself to her knees. Then she took hold of his arm with a frantic grip and almost pulled him down as she dragged herself to her feet. Dizzy, gasping, she still held on to South Boy to steady herself, whimpering the while.

During this time long-haired men—old men and middle-aged—had been filtering through the crowd to form a tight-packed, panting circle around the body. They jostled one another for first-rank position, like a pack of eager runners at a county race, and watched the policeman with expectant, half-hostile eyes, resentful of his interference but realizing that it was something they must put up with. Many of them were sobbing, and tears streaked every face.

The air grew so thick that it was almost strangling. It was a distillation of stinks, for the hysterical grief had added something new to the usual complexity of smells from sweating bodies. South Boy bore up under it as he bore up under the weight of the fat, whimpering widow—aware of his dignity and determined to maintain it as long as he could breathe at all.

The policeman straightened up, looked at the mirror, and showed it to South Boy.

"No breath," he said.

"No breath," echoed South Boy.

"Go ahead," called the policeman.

There was a rush of bodies that would have knocked South Boy to the ground but for the fact that he was firmly anchored to his rifle barrel. That which had been Yellow Road was rolled up in the blanket on which it lay, heaved up over the heads of the men who rushed it to the burning pile—now a platform of logs that filled the fire hole and rose three or four feet above the level of the mesa. They rushed through the wailing crowd that scattered to every direction before them—for nothing must stand in the way of the speedy obliteration of the dead.

The widow cast loose of South Boy and ran shrieking after the body.

A puff of wind stirred the air and sweetened it. South Boy gasped gratefully. With his third breath he smelt smoke and ran from under the ramada. Someone had already fired the thatch.

South Boy was thinking: If I could be like Joe, now, then I'd be something. He isn't cohiva-michiva no time, nor he isn't halfway one thing and halfway something else. He's *man* all the time. I got to talk to him more and get things figgered out."

CHAPTER XIII

THE ALYAH

AT THE TIME of the burning, the hidden sun had almost gone
down into Nevada. The gray of the day had darkened so that
the blazing willow-roof and granary cast a yellowish glow
over the mesa where people made their circle around the
place of cremation as mourners had done since the burning of
Mutavilya in the First Times.

The body had been promptly covered with logs. The fire
tender, an old man with frowzy gray hair, wearing only a blue
shirt, added the only modern touch to the scene when he threw
a can of coal oil over the logs, struck a match on his hard bare
heel, and leaped away to avoid the sudden burst of flame. The
cries of the mourners rose in pitch, and startling loon-cries
came from several points in the circle. Those that cried thus
publicly proclaimed the expectancy of their own early death.

But the most dramatic incident at Yellow Road's cremation
came with awesome suddenness out of the sky. A great ball
of fire rose from somewhere in Nevada, arched across the
valley and exploded with a scalp-twitching crash against a
black mountain in Arizona. There followed a whole series of
sharp detonations and long rumbling echoes.

No one seemed to give much regard to either the lightning
or the thunder. South Boy looked around the circle of
mourners and saw each one weeping after his own manner,
oblivious to the display overhead. He saw Havek, head down
on his folded arms. He saw Maria for the first time that day.
She wore shoes and a black dress. Her hair was loose, but it
was combed down smooth and straight and she was crying into
a lace-bordered handkerchief, like a white woman.

There were two people not in the circle. One was the policeman and the other was the woman with the new baby. They
were just outside, to the north, the woman sitting on a little
mound nursing her baby, weeping, talking, and chewing gum.
The policeman was standing up, looking around the circle of
mourners very intently.

South Boy, who yesterday would have joined the mourners,
ran over to stand with his friend the policeman.

The policeman gave his arrival no heed, but the woman
started talking to him right away: "I can't stand up and cry.
The baby pulls on me and my belly walks around a little yet—"

South Boy said to the policeman, "What are you looking
for?"

"The doctor's left. I told him to go. Now I got to see who's
fixing to take out after him as soon as the burning is over."

"You think they will do something, then?"

"Not if I catch 'em first," said the policeman. Then he added,
"How come you're not standing with Havek? He's over
there."

South Boy hesitated. "Well, he's a relative. The crying
women got him." He looked down at the woman and said,
"Does she understand English?"

"No. Too old. Never went to school."

"Well," said South Boy in as confidential a tone as the noise
would permit, "up there, up-river, we found a witch's pouch
that the Piute left. Havek went kind of loco. I got him down
to Hardyville and then down here. I had a hell of a time with
him. I think he's all right, but now that I have got him with his
folks I feel like I want to stay shed of him until I'm sure he's
all over it."

"You did all right," said the policeman. "You brought him
home. A lot of grown men I know would have left him and
run. Down-River-Old-Man told me about it. He said you did
well. He said he cured the boy of the witchin'. Is that right?"

"How do I know he was witched?" asked South Boy sullenly. "I think maybe the Mormonhater told him something that threw a big scare into him."

"Maybe the Mormonhater witched him. There's lot of stories being told around about that old man."

"Them's lies," denied South Boy hotly. "He may have scared Havek, but he never witched him. Fact is, I saw him pretty near sweating blood trying to unwitch him."

"Maybe, but I say Down-River-Old-Man unwitched Havek, and I'm going to stick to it. I'm going to tell Yellow Road's kin, 'Down-River-Old-Man was busy curing a young man of your family who had been witched by a Piute. That's how come he had to let the old man die.' That'll stop 'em. This business of Mojaves killing Mojaves is no good. Besides, it's against the law."

South Boy listened to the mourners for some time. Then he said, "Joe, you sure are smart. I want to go to Phoenix to school, or to Haskell, like you did."

The policeman turned and stared at him full-faced. "Hey, you can't! Those schools are for Indians. You ain't Indian!"

South Boy muttered, "That's right." He felt as though another door had been slammed in his face. The fog of doubt and uncertainty began to creep over him again.

It was then that he saw the alyah, which was a bad thing for him, in that state of mind.

The fire had burnt out its first eagerness. The wailing and shrieking of the mourners had subsided into a crooning, sobbing monotone of weeping. A sand devil rose up from the flats, gathered a whirling cascade of sparks from the ashes of the ramada and showered them over the mourning circle. One lit on the tahoma of a gaunt old woman. She threw it to the ground and stamped out the fire with big, bare, bony feet. The feet were a man's feet.

South Boy asked sharply, "Is that a woman?"

"Sure," said the policeman uncomfortably. "Sure."

South Boy said, "She looks like a man."

The woman spoke up. "That's an alyah. Don't you know anything?"

The policeman said angrily, "I thought you didn't understand English!"

"I understand 'man' and 'woman.' I think you lied to this boy."

"She's a woman on the agency rolls, all right," the policeman replied hotly. "How the hell am I supposed to know any difference?"

South Boy said: "I never saw an alyah before that I know of. I thought they were entirely of the Old Times." This last he said in Mojave for the benefit of the woman.

"They don't make them any more," said the woman.

The policeman's face grew taut with anger. "You're damn right, they don't. I'd like to catch 'em at it! We can't do anything about the old ones, but there ain't going to be any more of them."

"Who would want to make a woman out of a man?" asked South Boy. "That's nonsense—like making a burro out of a horse."

"It's the women," said the policeman.

"What's he saying about?" the new mother demanded; so South Boy repeated his own question in Mojave.

"Caw! This is how it happens. The boy is an alyah since the First Times. When he comes to the age for dreaming, he dreams he wore a skirt in Mutavilya's house. So his mother called in four alyahs, if there are four among the people at that time. Otherwise they call in enough old women who know the singing to make up the four. They sing all night over the boy while his mother and his grandmother make him a skirt. In the morning he puts on the skirt, dances four times around the fire and out of the house, and he is an alyah. I haven't seen it done, but many old people have told me about it."

"Ugh!" said the policeman, both embarrassed and angry. "Don't you go telling any white people about this! They love to dig up dirt about us. But I'll tell you the truth—it was the women who made alyahs.

"Take a woman who had an only son, or a youngest son she wanted to keep around her camp—keep him from going traveling or going off to live with some girl. She started working on him when he was still young, let him sit like a woman beyond the time when he should have been taught to sit like a man, taught him to think and talk like a woman and to do things that women do and to dread things that men do—like traveling and war. Then he dreams he is an alyah. Sure! The women have worked on him until he can't dream no different."

South Boy was silent, thinking this over.

Suddenly the flaming mass of the cremation fire broke in the middle. It sent up a great shower of sparks as it cascaded into the fire hole. The women began weeping bitterly again, crying, "Gone, gone, gone! Never-to-be-named. Gone, gone!" And the wailing of the mourners rose to a sharp, brief crescendo and then rapidly died away. The circle began breaking up. People gathered into little clusters or wandered slowly about, singly or in groups. The great bed of coals in the fire hole still glowed fiercely. Four men stood around it leaning on long-handled shovels, ready to fill the hole and carefully obliterate every evidence of its existence as soon as the coals were ashes.

One small group of men that had gathered together in a close huddle suddenly moved off towards the mesa's rim.

"Oh! Oh! There they go!" said the policeman softly. He jumped from the mound and ran for his horse.

"Joe!" cried South Boy. "Joe! Let me come too!"

The policeman shook his head and said without turning around, "No, I don't want no witness on this kind of a deal."

South Boy looked frantically around for someone, but the whole world was moving this way and that on its own business. He looked down at the mother. She was grinning and chuckling at her baby while the tears were still wet on her face. He caught a glimpse of Havek in a group of his younger relatives moving slowly toward the edge of the mesa—their heads low, still weeping. He saw the Whisperer and Maria and the poor relations walking away together. They would have welcomed him, but he could not bear the thought of Maria's sharp questions nor the sickening oglings of the fat girl. He looked for Heepa, his deputy-foster-mother, but she wasn't with them.

He was absolutely alone.

Everyone was going, and he couldn't stay in that place of death. Even the ashes of the shed and granary were wandering away, blown this way and that by the occasional purposeless puffs of hot wind. It was growing darker.

Panic-stricken by the thought, "They may have burnt *my* property!" South Boy ran to the place where the granary had been and there he found a bunch of sweat- and tear-stained schoolboys helping themselves to his traveler's rations and his canteen, for food and water are the property of the hungry and thirsty. But his cartridge bag had been carefully laid out of harm's way.

The boys immediately began shouting all at once. "Hey, South Boy! Hey, we pulled your stuff out from in under so they wouldn't burn it. Who gave you all the bullets? Le's see the gun!"

One of them hospitably offered him his own grub bag. He put his hand in it and finding no more than a fistful of corn and pumpkin seeds left, he prudently rolled the bag up and shoved it into his hip pocket.

The boys milled around him, shoving one another aside. "Let me carry your gun, South Boy. . . . No, me. . . . We heard you did a Great Thing up-river. . . . Did you shoot the Piute with that gun? Tell us truly!"

South Boy said, "No, I didn't shoot no Piute with no gun." He winced because he thought about the gun he'd forgotten. Then he said, to bolster his self-esteem, "He had this gun."

"Ah, ah!" shrieked the admiring chorus. "He took the gun from the Piute. A Great Thing!"

"Where did you hear about this business, anyway?"

The boys looked at one another and asked the source of the news; but no one seemed to remember who first heard it, nor from whence it came.

South Boy was thinking: How does such news always leak out among Indians? And how does it travel so fast? In this case Havek would have said nothing about the fight during the course of the morning, and Joe had had no opportunity to tell about it, even if he would. Yet these boys know at least something of it . . .

He tried to keep his mind busy with this puzzle as he moved off toward the trail in the midst of the milling mob of admirers who kept shoving one another to get close to him, quarreling over who was going to have the honor of carrying the big gun. South Boy said he would carry his own damn gun, but he gave the bullet bag and the empty canteen to eager hands.

On the way down the switchback trail the shoving got so violent that one boy nearly fell over the cliff.

"Stop it!" shouted South Boy. "Do you want somebody killed?"

Silently the boys fell into single file, some before him, some following. Last week they would have told him to shut up, or maybe pushed him off the cliff.

To his surprise South Boy found that he wasn't any too sure that he liked his new status. "Four days ago I'd have been skylarking and carrying on with the rest of them. Now I walk in their midst like an old man, and they look at me out of the corners of their eyes." It made him feel the more lonely.

To add confusion to this loneliness, there came again out of the back of his mind the question, Where? Where to? Where am I going?

By the time they were down on the flat the boys had forgotten the reproof from the "new man" and were shrieking at one another in English and school-jargon Mojave, in competition with the rolling thunder that was now almost incessant. There were no doubts about their destination. They were headed for a swim in the slough—down a trail that was only visible when the lightning played.

It was black-dark now, and out of the black, stinking stillness came a gust like a sand blast. South Boy bowed his back to a hail of sticks, sand, cactus burrs, and gravel. A bunch of mistletoe as big as a bushel basket ripped away from a dying mesquite and came sailing over his head with a great *swo-o-o-osh!* A chain of lightning illuminated a world in motion in which only a line of bent human figures stood still. It dissolved into blackness with a teeth-rattling, earsplitting crash. South Boy felt his face burn with anger against the wind that beat him. He wanted to fight something.

The boys were crying out all around him, half in pain, half in glee. Then the wind went as suddenly as it came. More distant lightning began flickering in the sky, and the boys started for the lagoon again.

Somebody said the wind had given him a worse beating than he'd ever got from the school disciplinarian. Another, whose voice South Boy immediately identified as belonging to a well known braggart named Sheridan, said that the wind was nothing. He was tough. He would stand against that wild wind stark naked. He was half joking, half earnest. The rest hooted and jeered and called him a liar.

Everybody was enjoying himself very much but South Boy, who had begun listening to what came from the back of his mind:

Am I headed back home? Will they put a collar around my neck and laced shoes on my feet, a satchel in one hand and a railroad ticket in the other? Will I live to come back? And if I do will I be wearing a black coat and carrying a Bible in my hand?

Again the air was dead and heavy. South Boy pushed through

it toward the lagoon. The lightning had ceased for the moment, and out of the limitless darkness he conjured up a picture of a young man in a black suit sitting on a red plush chair in a ranch-house parlor, talking to women about the affairs of women and drinking tea.

Who drank tea but women and preachers?

Then the real world flared up before him in a flash of light. He was standing on the bank of the lagoon. Others were coming up behind him, so he stood by, leaning on his rifle. His stress of mind goaded him to gather his possessions. The boy who carried the canteen came up. South Boy seized it and dropped it at his feet. The boy carrying the bullet bag came by. He seized it and laid it on the canteen. He stood there while the yelling boys tore off their clothes, or part of their clothes, and one after another jumped into the water.

What then is a preacher but a sort of alyah of the mind who is made to live in the world of women? thought South Boy.

Then, he remembered what the policeman had said: this business was the fault of the women—they taught him to think and talk like a woman and to like the things that women like and hate the things that men do. And he thought, All this business of Cultural Advancement and Christian Instruction—two roads that lead me into the world of women. And wasn't I warned plenty that the world of men is a Rough World and I should fortify myself against it?

Slowly he began to strip off his clothes, adding his shirt and overalls to the pile of his possessions. Then he snatched the handkerchief from his mud-caked head and threw it down. Well, nobody will make a tea drinker out of me! And he leaped into the lagoon, and the soup-warm water closed over his head.

For a long time he lay suspended in the water, spread out like a resting frog, slowly rising to the surface. Here I am between two worlds. I have no place. I have set my foot on three roads, and they have been blocked to me. If the fourth road leads to a black coat and a cup of tea, I'll leave it. I will go down the river to the Cocopah country where the deer are as big as burros and the wild pigs run through the brush like fleas through a dog's hair—where the lion, the spotted tiger, and the spotted cat live as in the First Times—

His head broke the surface of the water. He felt worse than ever, for there came to his mind the uprooted cottonwood rolling helplessly and hopelessly down-river . . . the Cocopa country . . . the land of the outlaw and the exile.

In the midst of his depression there came to him a trick by which he might open the road that led to the Phoenix Indian school. He would cross the river and borrow or steal some of the waterproof black dye used by the Chemehuevi basket makers. Then he would ride a log down-river to the Parker reservation and go live with Heepa. He would establish himself an identity as Heepa's son and later go and claim entrance in the Phoenix school where he would be among Indian strangers and not white strangers, where they turn out a policeman and not a preacher.

"So I set my foot on the third road again," he said, and swam toward the bank feeling much better, his imagination busy with the elaboration of this scheme.

As his hands struck the mud another sand devil roared overhead, blasting the naked hides of the boys on the bank, making them yell with real pain. The loudest yell was in the rasping, changing voice of Sheridan, the bragger. Someone said: "There's Sheridan who bragged so loud. Let's catch him and stake him out on the playa where the next wind will get him good! We'll find out if his hide is as tough as he says."

There was a rush of feet, a thud of bodies striking the earth, and an angry, frightened squall from Sheridan. South Boy jumped up on the bank and felt the first big drops of rain strike his face. "Cut it out!" he ordered. "Get your clothes on. When the rain comes hard, this will be a bad place."

One of the older boys said: "Surely. That's the truth! Two big arroyos run right in here." So the boys let go of Sheridan and began hopping around like kangaroo rats, snatching at scattered garments whenever they were made visible by the intermittent lightning flashes.

South Boy said, "If I'd had my eyes on the outside of my head I'd never have come down into this rat trap." He pulled on his shirt and sniffed the air when his nose came out. It was still hot, but there was a new smell to it that overcame the stink of stagnant water and rotting vegetation. "Yes, it's going to rain like hell."

His mind was easier, but his body was dog-tired.

The boys started chattering about who or what had caused the storm, and immediately someone suggested the doctor, Down-River-Old-Man, had brought it on out of spite.

Sheridan rasped out, "They should have killed him."

Someone said, "Who? Why didn't you do it?"

Sheridan said: "Caw! That's not my business. Let some old man do it."

Two or three of the boys spoke up, declaring that Yellow Road's kin should have killed the doctor before dark as they knew he would cause trouble for the abuse they had given him.

Sheridan said, "Aw, they're afraid!"

A great and continuous flash of chain lightning arced back and forth overhead, and there in the dazzling brightness stood Havek with his arrowless bow in his hand. He looked big, angry, and entirely his old self.

His voice boomed out, "Who says my people are afraid?"

Nobody spoke up, and the darkness crashed down with the thunder.

By the time of the next flash Havek had come closer, and there he saw South Boy for the first time. South Boy saw his eyes dilate and a shadow of the witching terror cross his face. The blackness covered them. As soon as the thunder died down South Boy said, "My friend—Hawk Strikes—my friend," as though he were addressing a distinguished man whom he had not seen in some time.

All around him he heard the boys murmuring, "His name—his name—he named his name."

When the lightning came again, Havek's face was strong and his voice proud. He said: "This is a rats' hole in a rain. What did you let them come here for?"

"That's what I'd like to know," said South Boy. "Let's get 'em out of it."

CHAPTER XIV

THE STORM AND GOD

THEY crossed a naked playa and then a wide fan of sand and gravel that the two arroyos had spewed out across the flat in past storms. The gusts of wind came in increasing frequency. They came crazily from every direction. There was no rhythm in their occurrence. Some passed overhead with a whooping rush and scattered trash on the hurrying line of fugitives. Some pelted their backs or tore the sand from under their feet and threw it into their faces.

Havek ran at the head of the line of boys, pushing the end of his bow through the sand before him. The place was called "Side-winders-sleep-here." Once he stirred one of the thick, vicious little snakes out of its ambush in the sand, broke its back, deftly picked it up on the end of his bow and flung it into the darkness.

South Boy brought up the end of the line—the place of the second-in-command on a dangerous trail. He sent word traveling ahead to Havek: "There's a rincon in the bluff where the mesa bends. That's a good place."

Word came traveling back, "That's good, if the wind doesn't come out of the west." As this message passed from mouth to mouth some words would be heard high and clear in a moment of silence, some would come strained and distorted through a rush of wind, and some would be blanked out entirely by the thunder or the rolling echoes that came after the thunder.

South Boy did not get the whole of it till it was shouted out by the boy ahead of him, who limped stolidly along—a mesquite thorn through his foot.

Two or three of the boys began to complain that the blinding flashes and sudden blackouts hurt their eyes. The irrepressible Sheridan raised his voice, insisting that it wasn't going to rain after all. "This fire play means nothing—"

South Boy sent word ahead: "Hardyville-old-man said bad rain coming. So shut up!"

Then the wind came out of the west, very suddenly and with devastating force, bringing rain mixed with wind-blown sand. Havek turned directly and ran east along the southern border of the wash, the line following him, running lightly before the wind.

The bluff of the mesa rose directly ahead and there was the arroyo's gap like a V-notch in a rifle sight. South Boy screamed with the wind, "There'll be all hell pouring through that place in a minute."

The answer came traveling back, "There's a trail on the bank that's out of the wind."

Two minutes later South Boy found his feet were on a trail that many feet had cut into the south bank of the arroyo in past times. It was fortunate that the trail was in the lee of the bank, for the rain shot directly off the top of the mesa in a hissing sheet, carrying loose top gravel whistling over South Boy's head to strike the opposite bank with the force of a stream from a hydraulic jack, tearing into the hard matrix and dumping a flood of mud and rock into the churning stream that was already filling the wash below.

There on the trail South Boy stood almost dry. A fine mist, sucked into the partial vacuum under that curtain of wind-driven rain, felt like sea-fog on his face. It was cold. He was thinking, This should feel good after such a hot day. But it was too cold.

He shivered, miserably, feeling all alone again, shut in by an impenetrable wall of sound. Slowly, heads down, like a file of ghosts, the fugitives from the storm moved up the trail in the eerie, pulsing light. One after another stopped, shouted to the one behind, then dropped to the trail and stretched out, belly down.

The boy with the thorn in his foot shouted to South Boy: "Havek says we're high enough. Lie down, so you won't get blown off into the arroyo when the wind changes."

South Boy lay down. He had a gnawing, sickening, uneasy feeling. At the next bright flash he looked over into the wash. The stream, boiling along twenty feet below, was already undercutting the bank. "Another rats' hole," he said. "I got to tell Havek." He went forward, dragging his rifle and all his possessions over protesting bodies.

Hardly had he gone ten feet when the wind changed and drove the full, suffocating force of the rain right into his face. There was no prevailing against it.

A vivid flash of lightning showed a boulder half the size of a flour barrel set in the bank four or five feet above him. Slowly he climbed up to it, realizing for the first time that he was badly spent. He draped his body over the rock, took out his clasp knife and began digging a hole back of it. When the hole was large enough he laid his cartridge bag and canteen in it. Then lying over them, with one arm over his rifle, he curled his body around the rock. It was still warm from long days in the blazing sun and felt amazingly comfortable to South Boy's belly.

The beginning of terror came during a lull in the wind when the boy called Sheridan suddenly got to his feet and announced that the rest of them could lie there like pregnant women. He was going back to the Fort and sleep under a roof. Several yelled to him that nothing could stand against the wind up on the mesa, but he started up the trail, stumbling over bodies, yelling he was a man who didn't fear the wind.

A blast came straight down the wash. Sheridan screamed and went down. It was black for a moment—South Boy could see nothing, but he heard the gravel whistling by like bullets. A stone the size of a pigeon's egg struck him on the shoulder. It hurt. Someone shouted that Sheridan had been hit on the head.

The next flash disclosed Sheridan thrashing about on the trail with Havek and another boy holding him down. When the thunder died away South Boy heard someone singing, the words rising over the rush of wind and the wash of rain. It was the ordinary singing—about the half-human creatures of the First Times, yet it was a death song. The boy who sang was "throwing away his dream" in expectation of death. The tone and the cadence carried his mood. Ahead someone began cursing the doctor, naming his dead kin, accusing him of causing the storm.

Then, all at once, everybody began singing, a strange discordant jumble of sound that beat against the roar of water and the wail of wind, pulsating as did the light with the crash and fall of the thunder.

The boys were throwing away their dreams, for the trail had caved in above and below.

So Death was there, and there was no use fighting against it. Final and horrible as is the Mojave conception, it was an understandable and natural thing. The old man, that doctor, surely, whose shadow had learned the formula that controls the forces of nature when God gave out knowledge in the First Times—he had released this blind fury. There was nothing to be done but throw away your dreams and curse this bitter, revengeful old man and hope that the living would kill him for his misdeeds.

South Boy knew this, the Mojave, way of thinking. It was clear and logical to him. So, fighting his fear, he tried to force this naturalistic fatalism into the back of his mind from whence his terror came. But it was forced out and brushed aside by a torrent of words that came out of that place and raced screaming through his head.

"Heathen! Heathen! No God to pray to!

"The price of sin!

"The anger of God!

"Hell! Hell! Hell! Hell-bent are the heathen!"

With these came bits of Bible quotations, snatches from sermons, imprecations of the tent evangelist he had heard in Phoenix, and his mother's bitter, oft-repeated warnings against the heathen world. And all this time the wind lashed his half-long hair about his streaming face.

He had let his hair grow long, and he had run away to live in the heathen world. He had doubted the Word. He had compared the men of God to the alyah because they drink tea after the manner of women. He had sinned—and long hair, the sign and symbol of the heathen world, was whipping his face.

Over all the other noise he heard his own voice cry, "O God, I'll cut my hair—I'll cut my hair!" And the wind died, then, as though it had never been.

After that he didn't remember anything, except once, much later, when he found himself down on the trail with two boys sitting on him. There was no rain, no lightning, no thunder. There was noise enough—the rush of water that still tore through the arroyo bed and the bumping and grinding of the boulders the water carried with it.

He stirred and complained weakly. He recognized Sheridan's voice: "How much longer have we got to hold him down? I'm tired."

Havek said, "Well, I got tired holding you, too, when you were hit on the head."

"Was South Boy hit on the head? I thought the stones had quit flying by that time."

"No, it's something else. Sit still. He's my friend, and I'm taking no chances of him falling down there and getting drowned."

Chapter XV

THE NEW DAY

When South Boy awoke the next time he was not sure he was alive, for a warm, heavenly sun beat gently down on his aching back and legs, drawing the pain from them. It was entirely different from the fierce, terrible sun of the desert summer.

The heathen lie, he told himself. They say Heaven is a cold, foggy place. So he lay there a long time, for that was the most delightful thing he could imagine doing. Finally he realized his underside was still cold and wet, so he rolled over. It was a painful operation. Every joint was like a gate hinge that needed oiling.

He found himself looking up at the crooked, green-brown, up-reaching stem of a greasewood bush. His eyes followed it up to its flat spread of tiny, crinkly green leaves, shining like emeralds in the bright sunlight. And among the emeralds were tiny dots of orange resin, like small gems no man has even seen.

Above the sky was the color of turquoise fresh-cut from the mines near Santa Fe. A cloud of fluffed cotton floated across it.

This is Heaven as it should be, he thought.

Then he heard somebody say in Mojave: "I knew the witching evil would strike you, too, sooner or later. That is why I came back to find you last night."

He glanced to the left and saw Havek squatting on the gravel, staring anxiously at him. "Do you feel good now?"

"Yes," said South Boy tentatively, not thinking it worth while to deny that he'd been bewitched. He sat up and said emphatically, "Fine!" Then he asked, "How'd I get up here?" recognizing that he was up on the floor of the mesa.

"The trail started caving in. So we carried you up."

"And the rest of them?" South Boy said this hesitatingly lest he be speaking of the dead, but Havek pointed in the direction of the Fort with his chin and said, "There!"

South Boy got slowly to his feet and stretched his arms high over his head. There at his feet was his rifle, a patch or two of fresh, faint, lightish rust to show for its wetting, the bullet bag, its thick greasy canvas hardly wet at all, and the canteen. He looked at them almost with indifference.

"Crazy weather's gone," he said. "The world's all young."

Neither spoke for some time. Then Havek said, "I'm hungry."

South Boy moved his reluctant body just enough to get at his hip pocket and pulled out the bag that contained the last remnant of his traveler's rations. Thereafter he counted each grain of corn and each pumpkin-seed kernel and gave exactly half of them to his friend. They ate, chewing excessively, as though those kernels were the last food in the world.

By and by South Boy said: "Once I hit my thumb with a hammer. It hurt terrible. The four days of crazy weather was like that. Then, when my thumb quit hurting, it felt awfully good all at once. Right now I feel all over like my thumb felt then."

Havek said: "Do you feel like traveling? I have business down at my mother's camp." Havek's face was calm, but his eyes looked eager like the eyes of a hunting dog whose master stands with a gun under his arm wasting time in conversation.

South Boy was amazed at the idea that anyone would want to go anywhere or do anything but lie still and soak up the delightful sunshine. Then he remembered that the pot would be boiling for Havek in his mother's camp and his clan-uncles would be waiting to sing for him. He said, "It's sure uncivil of me to delay you, but how am I going to get my legs to travel?" He pondered this question some time, but the problem kept slipping away from him as he dreamed snatches of daydreams as pleasant as any he had enjoyed in his childhood.

Finally the answer came to him.

"Get your horses," he said.

Havek looked surprised. "*My* horses!"

"What you took from the Piute is yours. Look down on the flat, on the V of high ground between the two washes. I bet they'll be there, by the big mesquite. Get your horses, and let's ride."

South Boy closed his eyes and drifted off into a sleep that was as soft as the cottony cloud floating over his head.

How long he slept, he didn't know; but when he opened his eyes Havek was there, sitting on the little stallion and holding the mare's lead-rope, saying nothing, but with the same eager look in his eyes.

South Boy thrust the heel of his left hand against the ground to force himself up. It sank deep into the once-hard mesa. When he was standing, he looked down at the print his hand had made. It was filling with water. For some reason he felt vaguely excited about it.

"The mesa's a sponge," he said, picking up his equipment and walking over to the mare, who promptly laid her ears back and showed her teeth. For the first time since he was a small child, South Boy felt helpless when confronted by a hostile horse.

"I just don't feel up to fighting her—not while I'm packing all this gear."

Havek rolled off the stallion and stretched forth his hand. South Boy gave him the empty canteen, stuffed the bullet bag inside his shirt, and balancing the woefully heavy rifle said, in Mojave, "I'm as heavy this morning as a woman eight months with child"; and he grunted as he heaved himself on the stallion's back. Still, he felt good, and he kept thinking about the water oozing into that hand-print as his horse swung over behind the mare and started off at a lope across the mesa.

The mare splashed through a pond an acre wide and three

inches deep. South Boy looked around him. Everywhere, all over the apparently flat expanse were those shallow, water-filled depressions—little lakes dotted with greasewood bushes like tiny green islands that glistened in the sun.

"There never was so much water up here!" South Boy felt his excitement growing.

"Why, the Indian wheat will be up as thick as the hair on a dog's back inside of two weeks!"

Then the momentous conclusion. "This mesa could feed twenty thousand cows and feed 'em fat, this winter!"

In an ordinary year the rain would have made little difference, for it always strained his father's credit to the utmost to buy the four or five hundred feeder steers for winter fattening on mesquite browse and alfalfa. But this year there had been a devastating drought in the high country in central Arizona. Word came that a hundred thousand head could be had at panic prices because the steers were too poor and weak to stand the harsh winter up on the plateau.

South Boy's father was there now buying the usual five hundred head that was all his normal feeding capacity could handle. He would pick and choose, traveling far, taking a few of the strongest and best animals from each ranch . . .

"To hell with that!" cried South Boy. "I got to get word to him about this mesa. Tell him to buy all he can as cheap as he can—anything that can walk. And to hell with giving the railroad shipping money. We drive. Every gully's full of water . . ."

The drumming hoofs of his loping horse began to beat out a joyous refrain:

> *We're gonna get rich!*
> *We're gonna get rich!*

So South Boy rode through the new, clean, wonderful world, with all the gray dust washed away and each mesa pebble bright with its own true color—as bright as the vivid red, yellow, purple, and red-brown of the distant mountains; but he no longer saw it. His mind was working like a ball mill on the problem of getting three or four thousand, or maybe even five thousand starved, frightened, weak, and wobbly long-horned cattle through those same mountains, where the trail was too narrow and too steep.

"By grab, we got to hold 'em and feed 'em up first," he said.

Before he knew it they were off the mesa and down through the wash where the smoke tree grew, down on the flat at the place called Aha-vel-pah, where the swale was now a small lake all around the three cottonwoods, where two killdeers rose on their long wings, screaming.

South Boy said aloud: "Well, that's a job for me. A swell job. A good arrow that kills two birds.

"I got a job for you, too, Havek."

Havek turned around on his mare and said, "Khootch?" politely.

"By damn, I'll make you rich, too. I'll get you a job that'll bounce dollars into your war bag."

Havek looked alarmed.

"No. I'm not crazy. I got a deal in mind. There'll be a holding-ground for you and me to keep, across the mountains . . ."

"No," said Havek. "My business is here." And he pointed down-river, toward his mother's camp, with his chin.

South Boy shut his mouth. Yes, there would be the boiling pot and the singing uncles waiting for him down there. He would sing his dreams every night for four nights, and he would be feasted at every rancheria where he had kin—clear down to Parker and below. He was a New Man who had done a Great Thing.

"I can see why a few dollars bounced into your war bag would not mean a thing to you now."

Then all at once it came to South Boy that he and Havek

had come to the fork of their trail. They would go on being friends, of course. But they would shake hands solemnly and awkwardly when they met and not know exactly what to say to each other.

Once there had been no difference between them. Last year, at the Great Cry—the annual celebration for the year's distinguished dead—they had sat together with the other boys, holding the feathered wands for the young-men-who-run. Next summer, when the celebration would be in commemoration of the great Yellow Road, with singing and running and "preaching" and a drama of great deeds, Havek would be a young-man-who-runs. South Boy would be sitting on his horse among the white men, just watching.

"You know," he said, thinking aloud, "there might be a halfway between. You might go to Phoenix and when you come back get a government job."

Havek had pulled down the mare to let South Boy come alongside. "You mean, like Joe the policeman?"

South Boy nodded hopefully.

"No. Too much white man!"

There was nothing much to say after that, and in a short space they came across the Yavapai year-around hand, lolling in a saddle on a big blue roan, looking scornfully at the muddy little Piute ponies.

South Boy said, "I won't take you out of your way no farther," slid off the horse, handed Havek the rope, and took the canteen.

Havek neither spoke nor looked back, but beat the mare into a run and eagerly disappeared among the mesquite. South Boy climbed up behind the Yavapai and said, "Get me home in a hurry."

Though it was midmorning, smoke was rising from the rusty stovepipe that thrust itself through the roof of the summer kitchen. The Foreman's best horse, mud-caked to the belly, wearing the Foreman's go-to-town saddle, stood by the door with drooping head and hanging bridle reins.

"Where's he been?" asked South Boy, sliding off the roan.

"To Needles for telegraphing," said the Yavapai.

South Boy said, "Good—he got the idea, too," and he dropped his gear by the doorstep and ran inside.

The Foreman was sitting at the far end of the table, a lank forelock drooping over his grim face and his mouth open to receive the thick chunk of bacon impaled on his fork. He looked up when he heard the door slam, his eyes widening.

"Where in hell have you been! You got my woman scared pie-eyed."

"To Hardyville, visiting," said South Boy, and added eagerly, "Didya get a telegram through? Didya tell him the mesa was just sopping? Didya tell him to buy anything that can walk and to figger on driving and saving shipping money? And what did the Old Man say?"

At this point the fat cook, who had covered her face with her hands and sunk silently into her rocker at the sight of South Boy, set up a shrill howl of relief. "He lives! Santa María-Jesús-José, the Baby lives! Merciful Mother, what would I have said to the *Niña* if he had been lost! Oh, the stinking hand of Judas that made me throw that pot . . ." She went on like that for some time, calling South Boy "the Baby" and his mother "the Virgin," very much contrary to fact, but according to the usual custom of Mexican servants.

South Boy paid no heed to her whatever but anxiously watched the Foreman's face. The Foreman had the look of one of those captive eagles often seen tied to a stump in an Indian camp—sullenly, bitterly resigned to defeat.

"You couldn't get through to Needles?"

The Foreman grumbled a sullen negative.

"Couldn't get across the river?"

"Couldn't get *to* the damn river! The whole lower bottom is a bog."

South Boy saw that the Foreman was about to lapse into one of his sullen, dangerous silences. They usually came on when he had tried very hard to do something important and had failed.

South Boy said to himself, Well, I reckon it's up to me. He reached for the coffee pot and poured himself a cupful of coffee without taking the trouble to sit down. The cook, making setting-hen noises, filled a plate full of bacon and grits and shoved it over in front of him.

"I bet you could get through to Topock Station, or maybe Goldroads. They got telegraphs at both places. Telephones, even."

No answer from the Foreman, who still chewed on the same piece of bacon.

"Hell, we got to get word to him," South Boy insisted. "You can live a lifetime and never get a chance like this again."

"Sure! Sure! And when the chance comes, the cards is all stacked against you. I start out at daybreak all full of vinegar, and then, about the third time my horse bogs down, it comes to me, 'What's the use! Suppose I do get to Needles? The line's down, sure. And how do I know I can get through to the Boss anyway? All I can do is to wire him care of the station-master at Ash Fork. How'd I know he'd ever get it? Maybe he's in Prescott by this time. Maybe a hundred miles down the Sandy—"

South Boy turned to the cook almost in panic. "*Tiene um botte pa'ya?*"

The cook hadn't understood a word of the foregoing conversation, but she knew her man's condition and its usual cure. "*Uhn—quisa—media botte,*" she whispered, looking apprehensively at the rigid, deep-lined face and glassy, far-staring eyes.

"*Traemelo pronto,*" urged South Boy, and he drank more coffee to warm his hope.

She stole away like a fat, frightened cat and came back with a quart bottle of whisky, dust-covered and more than half full —evidence that the Foreman had been sober a dangerously long time. Carefully she poured out four fingers in a water glass and set it in front of him.

There were minutes of almost stifling silence and immobility like paralysis. The Foreman sat like a statue of pale-eyed doom in a red-stitched black shirt and handlebar mustaches. Then his hand reached out for the glass, and he drank with one great gulp.

South Boy's sigh was like a small explosion. He began wolfing his neglected bacon and grits. The Foreman's pale eyes slowly grew brighter and milder, and the little sun-wrinkles around them relaxed and the granite contours of his face softened.

Finally he reached for the bottle and poured himself another drink. "What's the matter with me?" he demanded. "We can ride over to Goldroads, and if the wire's down, we can go on to Kingman and just keep pestering the operator until we do get the Old Man."

"Why, sure!" agreed South Boy.

"And I know another good reason why he can pick up a lot of stuff awful cheap. I got it straight that them big operators have decided they got to go in for better and fewer cows. Going to clean out all the longhorns on them high ranges. Going to stock whiteface in the spring. . . . Say, how much I got coming to me on the books?"

"Two hundred sixty-six dollars," said South Boy promptly.

"By grab, that ought to buy me a hundred head of starved-out dogies, and I'll have a hundred fat yearlings to sell in the spring!"

South Boy knew that the time had come for him to present the great plan he had thought out on the way home; so he drew up a chair and leaned across the table.

"Look! We can't shove that weak stuff across the mountains

all at once. We'd lose a lot of them, and, anyway, we'd have
to lay out a lot of cash money to hire a big drive crew. What
we ought to do is to have a holding ground over in the breaks
on the other side where there's plenty of desert browse that
ain't been grazed lately on account of no water near. Of course,
all the holes will be full now—"

"There!" exclaimed the Foreman, his face turning red with
sudden enthusiasm. "There! What have I been telling everybody? You're smart! You're turning out to be worth all the
trouble I've took in raising you!"

"And I'm the feller to keep that holding ground!"

"And I know just the place! A trap valley that ain't seen a
cow in ten years!"

"Listen to the rest of this idea! The Old Man operates the
buying end, and maybe with one extra hand shoves the stuff
along to the holding ground as fast as he can. Then you and
the Yavapai operate from here to the holding ground. I'll keep
busy cutting out the strongest stuff and you-all can come over
every four or five days and snake a bunch of 'em over the
pass—"

"That'll leave you a long time on a kind of lonesome job—"

"Yes, I figger up into November, anyhow. Way past the
time when a feller's got to go away to school."

"Oh, so that's it!" The Foreman thumped his fist on the
table and roared.

"Well, you got to have a man who can take responsibility
on that feeding ground, or you're going to lose a lot of dogies—"

"Sure, sure. Ain't no question about it."

"And here's another thing. There's six hundred dollars carried on the books marked 'school money.' So long as I'm going
to be busy over on the holding ground, why, the Old Man
can just as well spend that on panic cows. This ain't no time to
have money idling."

"Son, it won't take much talk to make the Old Man see that

kind of a proposition. I reckon he'll see to it you have a herd of your own to peddle in the spring when the market is right." The Foreman reached across the table and solemnly shook South Boy by the hand.

All this time the cook was fussing around making clucking noises. She filled South Boy's plate again, and he heard her saying: "Eat! Eat! For the love of God. You are a disgrace to me. You look like a half-starved son of the poor with that hair hanging around your face."

So South Boy's hand went up to his half-long hair and his face went blank, for he remembered then that he had made a bargain and had not yet fulfilled his part of it.

It was dark in his mother's room, and the thick curtains over the window, the adobe walls, and the door that had not been opened all summer held in yesterday's heat. The dead air smelt of dust and lavender scent. South Boy tiptoed in, found a pair of scissors in the sewing basket on the table and tiptoed out and down the bare hall to his own room.

Here it was light because the window had neither curtains nor blinds. He stood in front of the mirror over the bowl and pitcher stand. He seized a lock of hair between the wound-stiffened thumb and forefinger of his left hand and whacked it off as close as he could. The effect was not pleasing, but he went on, whacking away as best he might, all around his head.

Then he addressed the ceiling. "That's a sorry wreck of a haircut, but I reckon it'll hold up my end of the deal until I can get to Kingman. I'll keep my hair short and keep heathen ideas out of my head from now on. And if you remember, I didn't make no promises about not getting out of being sent away to school, so I'll take it kindly if you don't jim up that holding-ground job."

Then his eyes fell on the bullhide sandals still on his feet. These, too, were part of the heathen world. He kicked them off and shoved them under the washstand with as much of the hair as he could scrape up with his feet. He sat down on his bed—disturbing a thick covering of dust that had collected since he had last slept there in the early spring—fished a pair of worn half-boots with high, runover heels from beneath it, pulled them on his feet and went clumping back to his mother's room to replace the scissors.

The scent of lavender sachet brought tears to his eyes. She would be coming back soon, and he wouldn't be there. She would be bitterly disappointed, and she would be worried half sick because he was out in the breaks alone, with a bedroll, a stock saddle and a fire hole for a home.

"Well, I'm a man, and there ain't nothing she can do but get used to it," he said as he wiped his eyes on his sleeve and softly closed the door. "And it won't be near as tough on her as if she found I was dead, or turned Indian—or something halfway between, like the Mormonhater."

And before the hour was past he and the Foreman were riding east on the trail to Goldroads and Kingman. The sun warmed South Boy's back, and he was thinking of nothing except how comfortable it was to be riding in a saddle like a white man. He heard the quail calling back and forth; and through the mesquite from the direction of Havek's mother's camp came the distant sound of Mojave singing. Both were pleasant—neither registered strongly on his mind.

By and by the Foreman started singing in a booming voice, "Green grows the grass in the valley, oh." South Boy didn't join him. He couldn't sing, and he didn't care.

The mention of green grass started him thinking—We're gonna get rich, we're gonna get rich—in cadence with the easy gait of his horse, and, swaying gently to its motion, he dropped off into a sound sleep—like a baby in its cradle.